Rescued by the Highland Warrior

MICHELLE WILLINGHAM

THE MACKINLOCH CLAN

ISBN 13: 978-1-960198-07-5

ISBN 10: 1-960198-07-5

RESCUED BY THE HIGHLAND WARRIOR

Cover art by Frauke Spanuth, Croco Designs.

CONTENTS

CHAPTER ONE

GLEN ARRIN, SCOTLAND 1312

"**S**he means to rid you of your child, my lady," her maid Síla whispered in her ear, glancing down at the goblet on the table. "Do not drink any cup she gives to you." Celeste de Laurent, Lady of Eiloch, kept her face expressionless, though the danger was real. Now that her husband was dead, his younger brother, Lionel, stood to inherit.

But only if she did not bear a child.

Hs wife, Lady Rowena, meant to ensure that nothing would threaten her husband's inheritance. The goblet was likely laced with herbs that would force her to miscarry if she was pregnant.

"Leave us," Rowena commanded. The maid obeyed, but cast another warning look toward Celeste.

The cup held a spiced wine, and Celeste toyed with the goblet, tracing her finger along the silver rim. But she heeded her maid's warning and did not drink.

"You would do well to leave Eiloch," Rowena said, her face placid with a soft smile. "Marry someone else and give my husband the lands that are rightfully his."

"I have no wish to remarry." Celeste straightened in her seat, staring down at the dark wine. "I will remain here, as is my right."

"Why would you stay where you are not wanted?" Her gaze centered upon Celeste's waist. "You may be entitled to one-third of Lord Eiloch's property, by law. But that does not mean you must dwell here, within these walls." Her smile turned menacing. "There are other places within our property where you could go." *Other, less desirable places*, she didn't say.

"I may be carrying Edmon's heir," Celeste said, refusing to back down. "Until I know for certain, you have no rights at all."

Once word had come of Edmon's death, Rowena and Lionel had descended upon Eiloch like a swarm of locusts. The threat of a pregnancy was all Celeste had left to defend her right to remain in her home. Her hands went to her womb, silently praying that she had quickened with her husband's seed. A son might keep her safe from the circling vultures—but she worried about her own safety.

"Try to remain here, and I'll see to it that your life is a misery," Rowena warned. "You'll get nothing from us, and you'll live on the edges of our lands among the crofters." She moved in closer, her eyes dark with intent. "It will be just like your life, before you wed Edmon. Or have you forgotten?"

Celeste pretended as if she had not heard Rowena's threats. But even so, a chill ran through her blood, as she remembered the years of hunger and how she and her sister had huddled together for warmth on cold winter nights.

She gripped the goblet, as if she could absorb strength from the silver. "No, I haven't forgotten." She'd chosen this marriage to escape the memories.

"Edmon never should have married a woman like you," Rowena said. "You know nothing of what it means to be Lady of a castle."

Celeste didn't deny it. During her brief marriage, she'd tried to learn, but the complexities of governing the people and managing the rents had overwhelmed her. Edmon had no choice but to shoulder the responsibilities on his own. He should have married a rich Norman heiress, one who would have brought land and gold to his coffers. Instead, he'd chosen her, the daughter of a lowborn Scot.

Edmon had desired her, and she'd given up her freedom in return for the security he'd offered. Their marriage had been her means of escaping the poverty of her childhood, a way of keeping her sister safe.

And now, she might have nothing.

"You carry no child within your womb," Rowena predicted. "And within a fortnight, we'll know the truth."

"Within a fortnight, you and your husband will be gone from here," Celeste countered. "For I do carry a child."

"You could not possibly know that." Rowena poured herself a goblet of wine. "And when it is proven that you are not breeding, your sister will leave with you."

Celeste wasn't at all certain Rowena was allowed to force her from the castle, by law. But she would not put it past the woman to try.

"You would not want Melisandre to suffer, would you?" the woman continued.

Celeste stiffened at the threat. Her little sister was hardly more than three-and-ten. "She's just a girl."

"She is. And if you insist upon staying here, she will endure the same fate as you." Rowena's calm expression revealed no remorse whatsoever.

Melisandre was the only family Celeste had left, and she could let no one threaten her. Iron resolution stiffened her backbone, and she understood now, that everything depended upon her bearing a child. A child meant sanctuary, a means of protecting those she loved. It meant keeping her home at Eiloch and being rid of Lionel and Rowena.

But almost as soon as she envisioned the faint hope, a cramping sensation began in her womb. It was a harbinger of her menses, and in her mind, she envisioned Rowena's threats coming to pass.

God help her. If anyone learned of this, they would lose everything.

"Drink," Rowena bade her, raising her own cup. But Celeste stood from her chair, rising to her full height. She had little time left, but she intended to use every moment of it.

"Leave my solar," she demanded. "I wish to be alone."

"One fortnight," Rowena said quietly. "That is all the time we will grant you." She rose from her own seat, eyeing her. "And do not think to hide it when you bleed. My maids will know."

Only after the woman was gone did Celeste breathe easier. Her insides were cramping again, and she slumped down in her chair, wondering what she would do when the truth came to pass. She felt certain that there was no child at all. Fear iced through her, while she wondered how she could protect her sister.

There was no time to find another husband or hire someone to give them shelter. Their home was located deep in the mountains of northern Scotland, and there were no abbeys or convents to grant them sanctuary. She tried to think of a thousand different solutions, but only one would solve their problem quickly.

A child.

The word was a fervent need, encircling her mind. There had to be a child somehow. Wildly, she seized upon the realization that it need not be Edmon's. No one would know if it was given by another man.

You can't, her conscience railed. How could she think to lie with a man, simply to conceive a bairn?

But then, how could she abandon Melisandre, bringing her sister back into poverty? Winter would be upon them within a few more months, and Celeste didn't want to imagine being cold or hungry again. Then, too, her sister was sweet and softhearted, dreaming of the day when she would wed a nobleman. Edmon had promised he would arrange a betrothal when she came of age.

If it were left in Lionel's hands, it would never happen. With no dowry or marriage settlement, her gentle sister would have no husband at all. At least, not one with property or wealth.

And if their fates rested with Rowena, they would starve.

Choose a man to be your lover, came the voice of desperation. *Conceive a child and it will mend all your problems.*

Celeste lowered her face in her hands, holding back the tears. How could she even consider it? Aye, she'd lain beneath her husband and allowed him to touch her freely, as was his right. But to lie with someone else, to tempt him as Eve had, that was far different.

She wasn't sensual or sly enough to seduce a man. And if it were to happen here, everyone would know.

Leave, the insidious voice suggested. *Take a lover of your choice and return.*

Her cheeks burned at the thought. How could she even imagine it? She'd lain with no man except her husband.

But you wanted another, her heart reminded her. *And he wanted you.*

Once, that had been true, years ago. She'd been torn between two men...one who was the logical choice. And one who was her heart's choice.

Even now, she wondered what had happened to Dougal MacKinloch. She'd never forgiven herself for leaving him. And although she'd buried the pain, she feared that seeing him again would only reawaken the loss.

You did what you had to, her conscience reminded her. *For Melisandre.*

The slight creak of the door caught her attention, and her sister entered the room. Melisandre was too thin, her face almost hollow. She'd grown so tall in the past year, she hadn't had time to fill out. There were no curves on her body, and her fair hair was braided back so tightly, it made her blue eyes stand out.

"They took my gowns," Melisandre murmured, her voice barely audible. "Lady Rowena said—sh-she said I would not need them." Crossing her arms over the bronze silk she'd out-grown a year ago, her sister bit her lip. "Is it true, Celeste? Will they send us away?"

"I won't let that happen." She opened her arms, and Melisandre came into her embrace. Though her sister was nearly as tall as she was, she seemed far younger today, more vulnerable.

"She gave my gowns to her daughter," her sister confessed. "I didn't know what to do, and I could not stop them."

"You were right to come to me," she said, hugging Melisandre. The need to protect her sister was stronger than her humiliation. But she had precious little time left, and she would not allow Melisandre to become a victim. "Tell Síla that I have need of her." Her maid would help her to make the necessary arrangements for traveling.

Celeste could save both of them, so long as she put aside her misgivings and took a lover. Preferably someone she would never see again.

But she could not relinquish the memory of Dougal or the way he'd stared at her, as if she were his reason for breathing. She wanted to look into his dark eyes again and see the love he'd once felt. To go back to the years lost between them and lose herself in his arms.

He was her best hope now. Her only hope. "Everything will be all right," she promised her sister. "But I need to leave for a short while. We must seek help, and I intend to speak with some of the Scottish chiefs."

"They aren't our allies," Melisandre warned.

"No, but I will ask. In the meantime, I want you to remain here, and stay close to Síla." She trusted her maid to keep her sister safe.

"What about Lady Rowena? She might try to send me away." Her sister's face whitened at the thought. Though it was a real danger, Celeste strongly believed that if she left Eiloch, they would ignore Melisandre until she was found.

"Rowena is more worried about any son I might bear," she reassured her sister. "I won't be gone longer than a fortnight. Just try to stay out of her way, as best you can."

When the cramping shifted again, she felt the telltale presence of bleeding. She was not with child. But she would do anything in her power to get help, whether that meant taking a lover or finding someone to protect them.

And when it was done, she and Melisandre would be safe.

Glen Arrin, three days later

Dougal MacKinloch walked alongside the mare, speaking softly to her. So gray she was almost white, the mare stood fifteen hands high. Over the past few weeks, her lash wounds had faded into pink scars. He'd purchased Ivory only this past spring, and she'd been beaten and half-starved at the time. Each day, he'd tended her, trying to gain her trust after she'd been abused by the traders.

But she was his now. He'd spent every last piece of silver to buy her, for it was rare to find an Arabian horse this far north. He suspected she'd come from a Crusader knight, and he believed she was a pureblood. One day, if all went to plan, she would bear foals that could be trained and sold as warhorses.

He had never attempted to ride Ivory until today. As a bribe, he gave her a small carrot and led the mare across the glen, one hand on the bridle, the other on her back.

"We're going to take a short journey," he told her as she nudged at his face with her nose. "I'll be letting you run as fast as you like."

He touched her head with his, running his hands over her sensitive skin and continuing to voice compliments. Thus far, he had not attempted a saddle, and it was likely she'd try to throw him off when he climbed onto her back.

It was more dangerous to ride her with nothing but a blanket, but he wanted the mare to feel his weight, to know that his voice was the familiar tone she'd come to trust. She grew skittish when he mounted, but Dougal soothed her with a hand. Winding the reins around his palms, he nudged her with his knees, letting her move into a slow walk.

"You're going to break your neck," called out the voice of his brother Alex. As the chief of the MacKinloch Clan, his older brother didn't like anyone taking chances.

"I may." Dougal glanced back as the mare continued on her walk. "You can send men after my broken body, a few hours from now."

"She's not ready to ride," Alex argued. "You should wait until the end of the summer."

"You're wrong." And with that, Dougal urged Ivory forward, letting her increase the pace until the light canter turned into a gallop. He knew this horse better than anyone, and she had a need to run.

He'd named her falsely, he soon realized. She wasn't soft and pure, like ivory. This mare was more like a flash of lightning, for she tore through the meadow, running as if she'd craved this for months. Dougal held on with his knees and his arms, letting her take the lead. Never before had he gone this fast, and it was as exhilarating as he'd imagined. He let her go at full speed, never minding that they were miles past Glen Arrin and moving deeper into the mountains. The silvery loch gleamed behind him, and still the mare ran.

The familiar arms of solitude embraced him, and Dougal welcomed the isolation. He preferred being with his animals, for they had been his solace when his brothers, Bram and Callum, had been imprisoned. Although that had been many years ago, he'd grown accustomed to being on his own. His mother had been so lost in her anger, she'd forgotten she had a fourth son.

Because of it, he'd learned to rely only on himself. He could hunt when he needed to, fight anyone who dared to lift a blade, and he'd built a house with his own hands. He liked being alone, and it would remain that way.

The mare had begun to slow down, and he eased her into a canter and then a walk. Murmuring words of praise, he was about to dismount and lead her to water when he spied a small group of men in the distance.

The mare nickered, and his instincts went alert when he saw a woman on horseback. Her escorts moved forward, weapons drawn, and there was no question that a fight would break out. Dougal wasn't foolish enough to go closer without knowing who the men were or what they wanted. Yet, he was intrigued by the sight of the woman.

He drew his mare up the embankment, hiding them both among the trees. Ivory was skittish, uneasy about obeying him, but he continued to soothe her with his words and hands. Slowly, he guided her to higher ground. When they were within a short distance of the men, he dismounted and drew the mare into a walk. A small waterfall trickled down to a pool, and he tethered her to a tree, letting her drink and graze.

He crept toward the men, wondering if they were English or Norman. Although his brothers had their own lands and had many allies, they were always vulnerable to attack.

A horrified scream split the air.

Anger flared through Dougal, and he unsheathed two dirks, hurrying past the trees until he reached the hill above them. Below, he spied the men attempting to drag the woman from her horse. It didn't take long to realize that she and her escorts had been attacked, and the men intended to take her. Her back was to him as she fought, trying to remain mounted, while her horse reared up.

Two bodies lay upon the ground, the murdered escorts of the woman. Three other men remained, and when he caught sight of their faces, he recognized them as outlaws, fugitives from the MacPherson Clan.

Stealthily, Dougal eased his way toward them, both weapons raised in readiness. It had been several months since he'd fought, but his brothers had trained him well. He knew how to remain invisible and how to use the element of surprise to his advantage.

Strike swiftly before they know you're there, his mentor, Ross, had advised.

With that, Dougal lunged from the trees toward the first man, burying his dirk within the man's ribs, while dodging the swing of a sword. He took the reins of the woman's horse and ordered, "Ride!" Slapping the horse's flanks, he turned back to the other two. Armed with a blade in each hand, he watched their eyes, waiting for them to strike.

"There are better ways to find a woman," he warned the first. "Leave this one and go on your way."

"So you can have her, MacKinloch?" the other taunted. "Look at her clothes, fool. She's got more wealth than you'd ever dream of."

Their words meant nothing, for he'd hardly bothered to glance at the woman. "Then she doesn't belong with the likes of you, does she?" Dougal moved his blades, preparing to strike whoever moved first. Though he wasn't certain if they'd leave her, he was ready for a fight.

With a quick glance behind him, he was startled to see that the woman was huddled on horseback, hiding her face. Why hadn't she fled? Didn't she know that these men would ravage her, taking what they wanted, if she didn't leave?

The brief flicker in his attention was all it took for one of the men to strike, and Dougal's jaw snapped backward at the force of the punch. Rage coursed through him, and he unleashed his fury, glorying in the madness of battle rage. His dirks sliced through the air, seeking enemy flesh. He no longer thought about his actions but let himself fall into the familiar blur of fighting.

There was no MacKinloch better with a dirk than he. It was an extension of his hand, a lethal slash that allowed no man to threaten him. Not even this one.

For a moment, the outlaw stood motionless, his body in shock as a thin line of blood appeared across his throat. He stumbled forward before collapsing to his knees.

The other hesitated, and Dougal flipped the dirk in his palm, catching it again. "Are you wanting to join your friends in death?"

It was enough. The man backed away, mounting one of the horses, before he took off in terror. Dougal didn't bother following him. The MacPherson Clan could easily find the outlaw within a day or two, if he alerted them.

He turned his attention back to the woman, cleaning his blades before sheathing them. She was holding her veil across her face, as if trying to hide from him. Dougal seized the reins of her horse and demanded, "Why in the name of God didn't you run?"

Because you were the one I wanted to find.

Celeste wanted to bury her face in the veil, anything to keep Dougal from seeing her. Not like this. As soon as he recognized her, he would turn away. She needed more time.

Her heart was thundering in her chest, for she'd never expected to find him so quickly. Of all the men who could have rescued her, why did it have to be him? It was both a blessing and a curse.

The two years had changed him, and he was even more handsome than she remembered. Dark haired with brown eyes, he was a ruthless fighter, lean and powerful. His strong jaw held a hint of stubbornness, and his mouth was tight with anger. But he would be even more angry when he learned that it was her.

His arms were crossed as he regarded her, his brown eyes glaring. "Well?"

She kept her head down, still concealing her face. "I didn't know where to go," she admitted. "I—I was hoping to find the MacKinlochs. When I saw you, I thought you could escort me to your clan, since my men..."

Her words trailed off because she didn't know what to do about the escorts who had died trying to protect her. Inside, she was numb, for none of this had gone the way she'd intended. She'd journeyed northwest with her two guards, believing she could visit the MacKinloch Clan and ask for help.

"Should we bury them?" she asked, glancing behind with her face still veiled.

"The ground is too rocky," he said. "We'll burn the bodies, and I'll take you back home." He didn't even glance at her when he began walking up the hillside. Within moments, he returned with a gray mare, the most beautiful horse she'd ever seen.

He'd always been good with animals. If she didn't know better, she'd swear they understood him. The urge to touch the mare was irresistible, and Celeste dismounted to move in closer.

"Show me your face," he commanded.

Though she didn't want to, there was no choice. He would learn the truth soon enough. Celeste allowed the veil to fall away, afraid of what he would say. Dougal stared at her as if she weren't there. As if he were dreaming at the sight of her.

To distract herself, she ran her hand over the mare's head. "She's lovely." She caressed the horse's skin, smiling when the mare nudged her cheek.

"Aye, she is lovely." Dougal held on to the mare's reins, running his hand over her creamy mane. Celeste found her attention drawn to those hands, and a sudden ripple of uncertainty slid over her. Those hands had touched her, years ago. A bleakness centered in her heart, reawakening the wounds she'd thought had healed.

"Why did you leave Eiloch?" His voice had turned to ice, in silent rebuke.

"My husband is dead." She took a step backward, faltering as she considered what she must do. "It's not safe for Melisandre and me to stay there." At least, not unless she were pregnant with an heir. Perhaps not even then.

Risking a glance at Dougal, she saw that he'd completely shielded any expression. There was no emotion there, no hint of what he was thinking. Did he despise her so much, even after all this time?

"I need help for both of us," she admitted. "And... it seems I need an escort, now that my men are dead. I could pay you—" The moment she spoke the words, she realized her mistake.

"I want nothing from you, Celeste. Except, perhaps, to watch you ride away."

"I can't return to Eiloch. Not yet," she argued. Not until she had a means of protecting her sister.

"Then why should I help you?" *After you betrayed me*, he didn't say. But she sensed the accusation, nonetheless.

"We were friends, once." She mounted her horse again, hoping he would accompany her. Instead, he held his ground, watching.

"Were we?" He took the mare and led her up the hillside. Celeste didn't know if he was guiding her or walking away. She nudged her horse forward, following him. Dougal said nothing, nor did he turn to acknowledge her. There was a faint path etched in the grass that led through the woods. Sunlight slipped through the edges of the leaves, casting shadows over him as he walked. She didn't know whether he was deliberately taking her into the woods to remind her of the place where they used to meet...or whether it was safer. Celeste gripped the reins hard, trying to blot out the visions of the past.

She wouldn't let herself think of it.

When they reached a small clearing, he finally spoke. "I'll take you to my brother's fortress."

"Thank you," she whispered, dismounting from her horse. Though she had never been to Glen Arrin, she'd heard stories of how Alex MacKinloch had rebuilt it into a castle. "Do you live there now?"

"I returned, after you left."

Words sprang to her lips, apologies for the choices she'd made. But then, she wasn't sorry about her marriage. Edmon had been a good man, one who had given her the sanctuary she'd craved. Even if she hadn't loved him, he'd made her feel safe.

"Did you ever marry?" The question blurted out before she could stop it. As soon as she spoke, she wished she hadn't asked.

Upon Dougal's face, she saw the flare of resentment, and it only heightened her guilt.

"No." The words were clipped. "Take the mare for a drink of water while I tend to the bodies."

Celeste took the reins from him and guided both the mare and her own horse toward a small pool of water. She was grateful for the task, because it gave her a reason not to speak. But the longer the silence stretched, the more she realized that Dougal would never be the man to give her a child. Not after everything that had happened between them.

"Let me reward you for your help," she repeated. "I have silver, or possibly—"

"You could not afford my price," he retorted. "I'll bring you home with me, and my brother Alex can decide what's to be done with you."

She was left standing there as he returned to the bodies of the men. What did he mean, '*What's to be done with you*'? Was she naught but a sack of grain to be delivered?

There was no trace of the friendship that had once been between them or the man who had made her smile. Though she knew she deserved his anger, she wished there was a way to put it behind them. She wanted to begin again and forget the past hurts.

The mist surrounded her, and Celeste took a moment to calm her beating heart. For these next few days, she could pretend that there was no fighting over her husband's lands, that her sister would be safe from harm. And perhaps, she could conceive a child that would save them all.

The idea made her want to weep, for it seemed so impossible. If there was any other way, she had to find it. Somehow.

In the distance, she scented smoke from Dougal's fire. It occurred to her that they could not stay here long. The smoke would only draw attention to their location. When he returned to her side, she told him so. "It won't matter, once we're at Glen Arrin," he said. "If there are men following you, they won't intrude on my brother's lands."

"I don't want to bring fighting to your family." She lifted her gaze to his, taking a deep breath. "If you will keep Lord Eiloch away from me, I will stay only a few days. No longer."

"And then what?" His knuckles grazed the mare's face, rubbing her gently with affection.

"I don't know. I'll think of something. My sister needs me." She couldn't face that unknown future yet; not when she might lose everything.

Dougal's expression said he didn't believe her at all. "Running away won't solve your problems. It will only draw your enemies to you." His hands stilled upon the horse. "And this isn't our fight, Lady Eiloch."

Her mood saddened at his use of her title. "You called me Celeste, once."

There was the faintest flash in his eyes, so fast she barely saw it. But it was a hint of interest, one that gave her hope.

"That was before you became someone else."

Celeste studied his dark brown eyes for a long moment, wondering if there was any friendship left between them. It didn't seem that he would forgive her for the choices she'd made.

At last she turned back to the stream, cupping her hands for a drink. The summer air was warm, and some of the water spilled from her lips, down her throat. His gaze followed the water droplets, though he spoke not a word.

Abruptly, he turned and mounted the mare. There was no saddle, but he guided the animal back toward the east. "Come with me, then. If that's what you're wanting."

Chapter Two

Throughout the journey back to Glen Arrin, Dougal questioned what he was doing. He should take Celeste back to Eiloch where she belonged—not to his family. God help him, he'd never thought to see her again.

She was still the most exquisite woman he'd ever known. Her hair was an unusual color, a blend of fair strands and brown, almost as if polished wood were touched with gold. It was coiled into braids, pinned up on her head, and she'd discarded her veil somewhere. She wore no jewels, but her gown was made of finely woven wool, dark green like the leaves of the forest. Tall and slender, she carried herself like the noblewoman she'd become. In her blue eyes, he saw the way she was fighting back her fears.

He didn't know what had happened with her husband, but the bitterness of jealousy had not left him. She'd grown more beautiful over these past two years, her slender body transformed into a mature woman's. But she'd given herself to Edmon de Laurent. She'd made her choice, and it wasn't him.

Honor prevented him from riding away. But as soon as he brought her to Glen Arrin, he intended to leave her with his brothers' wives. Let them decide what to do with her, for he wanted no part of this woman.

She still affected him strongly, even now. It had grown worse when he'd watched her drink from the pool. One of the water droplets had slid over her pale skin, beneath her gown. The wool clung to generous breasts, and he had to shut off his imagination to keep the unbidden desire under control.

Why in the name of God had she traveled here? He didn't doubt that there was unrest after the death of her husband, but didn't she realize how dangerous it was? Although he and his brothers had kept the English at bay for many years, there were always raids from neighboring clans or English soldiers who entertained themselves by attacking their fortress.

A beautiful woman with only two escorts was open prey. She wouldn't last an hour out here alone. He led her through the valley, noting the determination on her face.

But even more disconcerting was the way she kept glancing over at him. Almost as if she was trying to discern how to heal the broken years between them.

He didn't trust her at all. There were secrets beneath that treacherous face, and she wanted something—wanted it badly enough to run away from home. And it wasn't merely an escort.

They rode for hours without speaking as they drew closer to Glen Arrin. The castle wasn't large, but it was enough for clan gatherings. Although Alex had offered him a chamber of his own within the main dwelling, Dougal preferred the house he'd built on the outskirts.

Celeste slowed the pace of her horse as they approached, her eyes widening at the sight of Glen Arrin. When they rode through the gates, the castle towered high above the stone walls, an imposing structure that would defend them from all enemies.

"It's much larger than I thought it would be." She took in the sight of the structure, adding, "I heard that it burned down years ago."

He nodded. "We tried to keep to ourselves after we defeated the English. Our peace was hard won."

Although they'd paid the price in blood, he didn't believe for a moment that the truce would last. King Edward would rise up against the Scots, and Dougal and his brothers had no choice but to be ready.

His brothers had gained control of this region, and the MacKinloch Clan held great power. Still, they never ceased the endless training, the preparation for a battle that could be brought to their gates. Allies were necessary to their survival, and he suspected that his brother would want to learn more about the upheaval at Eiloch.

For a widow, Celeste did not appear grief-stricken over the death of her husband. Instead, she seemed far more disturbed by the prospect of harm coming to her sister. Dougal tucked that thought away as he led her inside.

He didn't miss the startled looks on the faces of his kinsmen. A few sent him sly smiles, as if he'd plucked the woman from the ground like a delicate flower. They didn't know anything about her, or the years he'd courted Celeste at Locharr, where they'd met. To them, she was a stranger, and he was grateful for that.

He led her through the inner bailey, directly toward the castle. Nairna, Bram's wife, caught sight of him, while she held the hand of her young niece. In her other hand was a comb, and the girl sent her aunt an indignant look.

"Have you brought a visitor with you, Dougal?" Nairna asked. She smiled warmly at the pair of them, but he didn't miss the gleam in her eyes. She had been trying to find a wife for him over the past year. He'd ignored her efforts, avoiding the women as best he could. Yet, he knew exactly what Nairna was thinking.

And he had no intention of letting her draw false conclusions. "Lady Eiloch has asked for our protection over the next few days. She can tell you more about what's happened." He reached up to help Celeste dismount, but the woman was staring at him, her mouth set in a frown. "I'll be with the horses."

He didn't give either of them a chance to argue but seized his escape. With the reins in both hands, he retreated to the stables. Better to leave Celeste with Nairna and the other women, where he wouldn't have to look upon her face or question what she truly wanted from him.

It was as if he'd been so eager to get rid of her, he couldn't leave fast enough. Celeste wasn't surprised by Dougal's retreat, but it left her feeling uneasy.

"Don't be worrying yourself about Dougal," the young woman said. "I think you made him nervous. I am Nairna, wife of Bram MacKinloch. And this is my niece Ailsa, who has not yet learned to comb her hair, it seems." She held up the comb, and the brown-haired girl eyed it as if it were a weapon.

"Aunt Nairna, please," the girl moaned.

"Either do it properly, or you'll bring shame upon your parents." She handed the comb over to the girl, gently guiding Celeste to follow her. "We are fostering her while Callum has my boys. Callum is Dougal's older brother." All the while she guided her inside the castle, Nairna kept talking, her bright voice filling up the awkward space.

But when they entered the Hall, Celeste was caught spellbound, her feet no longer able to walk another step. Above them was a round window made of colored glass. It was a depiction of the Madonna holding an infant child with bold colors of sapphire and emerald shining through like jewels. It took her breath away. She'd only seen one window like it, in a cathedral when she'd journeyed south to Edinburgh with her husband.

"Our chief's wife, Laren, made that," Nairna said. "It's beautiful, isn't it?"

Celeste nodded. But the image of the Holy Mother cradling a child struck her hard. Would she be holding an infant of her own by next spring? Or would she and her sister have to fight Rowena for her share of the land?

She knew the simplest solution was to conceive a child, but every part of her conscience railed at the idea. It wasn't right to use Dougal in that way. Her idea had been born of desperation as a last effort to protect her sister and herself. But it was wrong. And now, she didn't know what to do.

If there was any other way, she would have to find it quickly.

Nairna led her up a winding stone staircase that led into a small solar. There, Celeste found a red-haired woman sitting beside the window, dipping her quill into ink as she drew shapes. An older girl sat beside her, the young face intent upon the drawings.

"Are you teaching her your secrets?" Nairna said in a teasing voice. Nodding toward the woman, she said, "This is Laren, who made the glass you admired. And her eldest daughter Mairin." Turning back to Celeste, she added, "This is Celeste de Laurent, the Lady of Eiloch."

Laren glanced up, and a slight frown marred her lips as if she'd recognized the name. Swiftly, she recovered and asked, "Are there other visitors with you, Lady Eiloch?"

Celeste shook her head. "My men were attacked and killed on the journey here. Dougal saved my life, and I owe him my thanks." She studied Laren for a moment, wondering if the chief's wife knew of her. But if she did, the woman said nothing at all. Celeste didn't know whether to be glad of it or dismayed that Dougal had never spoken of her to his family.

"I am in need of help," Celeste continued. "Not only for me, but also for my younger sister." Her gaze centered on the older girl, whom she guessed to be slightly younger than Melisandre. She explained to the women about Rowena's intent to force them out. "I can't let that happen," she finished.

"Then why did you leave her behind?" Nairna asked.

"Their anger was directed toward me, not her. They did not wish to give up my widow's portion, when Lionel de Laurent inherited my husband's lands. I left Melisandre with my maid. I trust her to take care of my sister until I return." She felt uneasy explaining all this to the women.

"I will speak to my husband and ask what can be done," Laren said, setting down her quill. "Dougal may be able to accompany you back to Eiloch, to bring your sister to safety."

Nairna sent Laren a conspiratorial smile. Abruptly, she asked Celeste, "Did you find him handsome?"

She blinked at that. "Well, yes, but—" *He meant far more to me than that*, she wanted to say. At the pleased look on Nairna's face, she found herself unable to say any more.

"Nairna, don't," Laren warned. To Celeste, she added, "We will hold a feast this night to welcome you to Glen Arrin. It has been some time since we've had any visitors. And our husbands will discuss how to help you."

"And how we can coerce Dougal into being your protector," Nairna said. "He's been alone for far too long." She beckoned to Ailsa, taking the comb and guiding it through the girl's tangled hair. Deftly, she braided the strands, tying it off with a bit of thread.

"It's too soon for that," Laren argued. "She buried her husband only a short while ago, Nairna."

The woman sobered, her hand coming up to rest on her throat. "You're right, of course. I spoke without thinking." Her face had gone pale, and she admitted, "I would die if anything happened to Bram. Please don't be upset with me."

"My husband and I were friends," Celeste said. "I'll miss him, of course, but the marriage was arranged." Truthfully, she had not thought of Edmon a great deal. Aside from sharing meals and a bed with him, he'd been too busy overseeing the estates.

She had felt like an old cloak in many ways—there when he needed her, but Celeste didn't delude herself into believing Edmon had ever cared about her. He'd wanted her as a possession, not someone to love. Now that he was gone, she felt a slight sense of loss, but it was not heartrending.

What troubled her more was Dougal. She felt as if she were walking upon a barely frozen lake with him, afraid of taking any misstep. It wasn't clear how he felt about her, and she was wary of saying the wrong thing.

"Don't be embarrassed by me," Nairna apologized. "I tend to speak my mind and ask the questions I want to know. You needn't answer anything that makes you uncomfortable."

"She'll find out the answers anyway," Ailsa remarked, under her breath.

Nairna smiled at her niece, but her eyes gave a warning. Waving a hand, she ordered the girls out. "Go and begin the preparations. The men and women can bring foods to share, and we'll have music as well."

When the girls had gone, Celeste steadied her nerves. Tonight, she would confront Dougal and learn whether he was willing to help her. If he refused, she could speak to some of the other men. Although she hadn't the least idea of whether anyone would want to assist her, she had to try. Gaining the support of Nairna and Laren would make it easier, if she could find the right way to broach the subject.

An idea struck her, one that might work. Although it meant stretching the truth, it was better than the alternative.

"I wonder if you could help me," she began, feeling humiliated by what she must ask. "There is . . . another way I could protect my sister. If I were to find someone appropriate to marry."

As she'd predicted, Nairna warmed to her suggestion. "There are many unmarried men among the MacKinlochs," the woman agreed.

Laren held up a hand, intervening, "But you're wanting a nobleman, are you not?"

"I want a man who can keep us safe," Celeste answered, trying to hold to the truth as much as possible. "And I don't wish to be a burden upon anyone." She crossed her arms, feeling embarrassed by the confession, though it was true.

The two women exchanged looks. "Dougal is unmarried and he's quite good at keeping a woman safe," Nairna suggested. "But there are others who might suit, as well." Without letting her answer, the woman studied Celeste. "The women like Dougal because he's handsome and quiet. They won't be glad of your arrival, I can tell you that."

Celeste made no reply, though she wasn't anticipating the interference of other women. "Could you help me find some possible candidates? And tell me what should I do to attract the right sort of man?" Her cheeks burned at the lies she was speaking, though likely they would believe she was simply embarrassed.

The truth was, she couldn't imagine flirting the way other women did. She didn't know how to smile in a way that drew a man to her. Even the idea of trying to seduce one was horrifying.

Nairna tilted her head to one side. "The gown you're wearing is nice enough, but you need something to help you. She went into a small chest and brought out a golden necklace with colored green glass as a pendant. "Wear this."

She fastened the chain around Celeste's neck, and the pendant fell just between her breasts.

"Perfect," Nairna pronounced. "It will draw his attention in the right direction." When Celeste gaped at her, Nairna laughed. "Don't look at me like that, Lady Eiloch. You were married. You know where the men will be looking."

She reached for the pendant, feeling even more disconcerted by all this. Laren was the one who saw through her nerves and added, "Unless her marriage was not a good one."

Nairna's smile faded. "I'm sorry. I didn't think of that."

Celeste let out a slow breath. "Our marriage was much the same as any other. He desired me and our union was good enough."

"Did you love him?" Laren asked. The woman's voice was soft, sympathetic in her tone.

There were no true words to describe it. Edmon had been a reasonable husband, and he'd shared her bed each night. Their marriage had been comfortable.

"No, I didn't love him," she said at last. "But he would understand that I must do whatever I can to protect my sister from harm."

Nairna came behind her with a comb in her hand. Slowly, she began unfastening the braids, loosening the strands until they hung in waving curls down Celeste's back. "Do not cover your hair tonight, and do not wear it up." She combed through the strands, and then arranged them over Celeste's shoulders. "If you see a man who interests you, let one of us know, and we will help."

Nairna turned to face her. "I don't know you at all, Lady Eiloch. Thus far, you seem like a good woman. But I should be warning you—" she lowered her hands to her sides, her eyes turning serious "—treat our men with care. They are strong warriors, who would die for their women. We would do the same for them."

At the feast that night, the mead was poured freely, as fast as the men and women could drink. Dougal remained apart from the others, watching as his brothers' wives introduced Lady Eiloch to several men of the clan. Although it was likely that Nairna and Laren meant nothing by it, Dougal found himself unable to take his gaze from her.

Her hair was down, falling in waves past her hips. Nairna had loaned her a glass necklace, and Dougal didn't doubt that every man was staring at the place where the pendant was nestled. Those who were even more drunk would start fights amongst themselves for a chance to be with her.

It wasn't his concern. Why should he care if his kinsmen wanted to steal a moment away with Celeste? She meant nothing to him anymore. He intended to return to the horses, taking his leave from the crowd.

And yet . . . his feet would not move. It was as if an invisible spell had woven itself around him, making it impossible to do anything except watch her. Celeste stood surrounded by men, and yet, she stole a glance at him as if pleading with him to save her. Although she'd managed a smile toward his kinsmen, he could see her discomfort growing. She picked at her food, refusing several who asked her to dance. He knew, even if they didn't, that she hated dancing.

Dougal finished his own fare, but it was tasteless. Even with the sweetness of the mead to wash it down, he took no pleasure in the feasting.

"I never thought you were a coward."

Dougal turned and saw his eldest brother, Bram, standing behind him. He didn't know what his brother meant, but he suspected it had much to do with his avoidance of Lady Eiloch. "She's fine enough on her own."

"She doesn't want those men, despite Nairna's efforts to make a match. Her attention is on you. Why do you not go and speak with her?"

Because she made her choice.

Dougal felt the suffocating tension rising up inside him. Seeing her among his family was abrading his mood, making him wish they would all leave him alone. "She wants my protection, nothing more."

"Then you're blind, lad."

He bristled at that. He wasn't an adolescent lad anymore, but a man grown. "I've better things to do." Like drink himself into a stupor, to forget the way it had felt to be in her arms, to taste her lips.

"You're afraid of her," Bram predicted. His brother was baiting him, but Dougal refused to play any part of this game.

"I'm afraid of nothing. Especially her." He strode across the crowd, his mouth tight with anger. There was only one place he wanted to be right now—far away from the prying eyes of family members.

As if in answer to his dark mood, many women smiled at him as he passed. Several were fair of face, but he ignored them all. As he drew nearer, Celeste's eyes never left his.

His feet stopped moving, though he'd wanted to keep going. She was staring at him, a silent question in her eyes. He knew how much she hated people watching her. Like him, she wanted to be apart from everyone else.

Don't, his mind warned. The best course of action was to keep walking to leave her behind. Hadn't he learned anything since the last time?

And yet, he held out his hand to her. She took it without question, following him away from the MacKinlochs. Her hand was cool in his, the skin softer than he remembered. She said nothing at all but continued to walk with him to the stables.

"Thank you," she said at last. "I was feeling overwhelmed around so many people." She released his hand, even as she continued to walk alongside him. The evening was warm, and the scent of her skin caught his attention with the faintness of flowers. Her hair spilled over her shoulders, brushing against his hand.

In his mind, Dougal wanted to press her up against the fence, forcing her to admit that she'd chosen to wed the wrong man. He craved her kiss, and he wanted to touch more of her bare skin. But he pushed the errant thoughts away.

He stopped before the fence that enclosed the clan's horses. Ivory trotted closer, likely expecting a carrot or a piece of dried apple. But instead of coming to his side, she stopped before Lady Eiloch.

"You're a sweet girl," she murmured, rubbing the mare's nose. "I can't imagine that anyone would want to hurt you."

"Is that why you ran away?" Dougal asked quietly. "Was someone trying to hurt you?"

He hadn't thought of it in that light, but she'd left so quickly, it was possible. The idea of another man trying to claim her made him tense.

Celeste nodded slowly. "And because I need help." Her gaze fixed upon him, and suddenly, she reached out to touch his shoulder. "If you're willing."

The word *willing* slid through him with an entirely different meaning. He opened the gate and moved away from her, using the mare as a means of repressing the desire she'd conjured. Did she even understand what she was doing? Was she trying to push him closer to the edge?

"Why would I be?" Without waiting for an answer, he went inside the stables and brought out a brush to tend to the mare. Though he'd already taken care of Ivory earlier, he was looking for any distraction.

"Because I think I know something you do want." She opened the gate, following him. "And it's something I could give to you."

Violent heat roared through him. His lust-filled imagination provoked him with images of her silken skin, her eyes filled with desire.

And yet, when he turned to her, he saw naught but innocence in her eyes.

"Go back to the others," he warned. She had no idea how much he desired her, how his control was stretched to breaking point. "I want nothing from you."

"I meant only—" Her fingers touched his, and that was all it took to snap the thread of restraint. Dougal pressed her back against the wooden fence, his hands around her waist. Leaning in, he snarled, "I'm not feeling very honorable right now. I said you should go."

Most women would have fled at that very moment. She looked frightened, but instead of leaving, she whispered, "I would offer you a horse. A stallion to breed with your mare."

Her words penetrated the cloud of desire thrumming in his veins. A horse, she'd said. Not herself.

"There are no Arabians this far north."

"My husband had one," she murmured. "It was given to him last year. He's black, with a white star on his forehead."

"Is that what you think I want?" He had to know her purpose, and from the sudden confusion on her face, he suspected it was.

"Isn't it?" The question hovered between them, and when her lips pressed together, he grew suddenly aware that she had not tried to push free of him. Instead, she'd remained trapped in his embrace, as if she, too, wanted him.

"Your mare is important to you," she whispered. "I only thought you might want another horse like her."

"The horse isn't yours to give," he warned. No one alive would let a valuable war stallion go, not because of a woman's wishes.

"I keep my promises," she said. "And if you will help me find a way to keep my sister safe, the horse will be yours. If you want him."

Her hands moved to rest upon his chest. Aye, he did want a horse to breed with Ivory. She was a lovely mare and would make a good dam, with the right sire for her foals.

"Why me?" he demanded. "Such a horse is worth more than a chest of silver." That, he knew well, for he'd paid nearly that much for Ivory.

"What I would ask of you is not an easy thing." Her hands came up to his face, as if there were not two years of distance between them. As if she'd conjured up the past, reminding him of how she'd ensnared him.

The soft caress was his undoing. Pressing himself close to her, Dougal growled, "You don't ken what you're doing, lass."

"No," she whispered. "I know exactly what I'm doing." And she lifted her mouth to his, kissing him softly.

From the moment Celeste kissed him, she tasted the tension in Dougal's body. Like a frosted pane of ice, he didn't respond to her kiss at all. Her cheeks burned, for she'd thrown herself at him, only to find that he didn't want her. Her embarrassment went so deep, she was drowning in it. She pulled back immediately, wishing she'd never given in to impulse.

There was no love remaining within him. Not even desire, it seemed.

"What was that for?" he demanded, his face rigid. In his dark eyes, she saw suspicion and a glimpse of a man who would not allow anyone to break past his invisible boundaries.

"I'm sorry," she whispered. "I—I thought—"

I thought we could go back to the way it was before. But how terrible was it to find that he didn't desire her? That she had misread him and was wasting her time with a man who would not yield to a moment of madness?

"You were wrong, Celeste." His voice slid over her with the dark trace of danger. She expected him to release her, to push her aside even. But instead, he kept his hands on either side of her, leaving her trapped against the fence. She lifted her eyes to his, and in his expression, she saw wariness.

"You tempted me," she admitted. "I wanted to know if it would be the same as before."

But it wasn't. Not anymore.

Dougal used his height to intimidate her, and she grew well aware that this man was not one who would let a woman make demands of him. His dark hair hung below his shoulders, and though he was lean, she sensed that every inch of him was hardened with muscle. If she tried to seduce him, he would be very different from her husband. The thought sent a prickling rush through her skin. "It will never be like it was before."

"I'm grateful to you for bringing me to safety," she said quietly. "The kiss was my mistake, and it won't happen again." She expected him to back away from her, now that her pride was shattered into a thousand pieces.

But instead, he held her there, his dark eyes discerning. It was difficult to keep her thoughts clear when he was watching her like this. She turned her gaze aside and saw that the mare was grazing behind Dougal, the moonlight reflected against the animal's silvery coat.

"I meant what I said, about giving you the Arabian stallion," she added. "But if you want nothing more to do with me, I'll understand." She kept her gaze averted, not wanting to see his refusal.

"I'm not as daft as you think I am," he said in a low voice.

"I never said you were." Somehow, she'd triggered his anger, and she wasn't certain how to soothe him. But she was entirely aware of the way his arms rested on either side of her, his body shadowing hers like a predator.

He held her imprisoned, his face resting against hers. "You're wanting something else from me," he predicted, lifting her chin. "Something you won't tell. I know you better than any other man here. But I'm not one to be swayed by sweet words and soft kisses."

"Nor horses, it seems." She couldn't tear her gaze from him, and the touch of his hand warmed her skin. "Just let it be, Dougal. I won't ask anything of you anymore." She turned her cheek and pushed his hand aside.

"Did you ever kiss your husband like that?" he demanded.

Blood rushed into her cheeks, and she wondered why he was asking such a thing. Why would he care? "Edmon didn't like kissing."

If she didn't know better, she'd swear the answer pleased him. His shadowed face was unreadable, and she didn't know what he wanted from her now. She was about to demand that he release her, when this time, Dougal leaned in again.

"Was I the only one, then?"

Her heartbeat shuddered, and she was held captive by his deep voice. "Your kiss was the only one that ever mattered."

His arms encircled her waist, and she didn't stop him when he leaned in to claim her mouth. The kiss began with heated breath, firm and coaxing. She was lost in the touch of his mouth while his hands rested upon her hips. His mouth offered an invitation, not a conquest. When she opened to him, kissing him back, it transformed entirely.

Memories poured through her, of the way he'd taught her to kiss. Of the stolen moments when they'd practiced with each other.

She couldn't breathe, couldn't hold a clear thought while his hot mouth was upon hers. Heat pulsed through her body, her blood awakening as his mouth slid against hers. Bold and unrestrained, his tongue thrust against hers, demanding her surrender.

Without understanding why, her arms moved around his neck, and his hard body pressed against hers. She could feel his arousal against the juncture of her thighs, and the pressure wasn't at all frightening. Instead, she curved against him, welcoming his strength against her softness. Between her legs, there was an aching emptiness.

Desire. Need like she'd not experienced before was there in the way his tongue moved within her mouth. She wanted him to bare her skin, to feel his mouth kissing her everywhere. A shudder rocked through her when he rubbed himself against her.

When he released her, his dark eyes were raging. "Stay away from me, Lady Eiloch. Unless you plan to finish what we started."

With that, he strode away, leaving her with weak knees and a pounding heart.

CHAPTER THREE

With burning cheeks, Celeste moved back to the crowd of MacKinlochs. There was music and she saw the chief, Alex MacKinloch, with his wife, Laren, seated beside him at table. He leaned over to whisper in her ear, and the woman blushed, sending him a secret smile.

All around were men and women stealing away for a moment alone. Even Nairna was dancing with her husband, Bram, their eyes locked on each other.

Celeste stood back from them, feeling as though anyone could see the guilt on her face.

Now she understood why he'd kissed her. Dougal wanted retribution for the way she'd left him. He wanted to remind her of the passion between them, showing her what she'd turned away. And he would be the one to leave her now.

Dougal might be willing to take her into his bed—but not as an act of love. She felt certain he would use it as vengeance against her. Was there another way out of this, other than returning with a child in her womb? It was such a desperate act, and there was no guarantee that she would even give birth.

Especially with Rowena plotting against her, wanting her to miscarry. And once again, she understood that her reckless plan wasn't right or fair. It was better to find another way of protecting Melisandre. But how?

She would have to fight for her share of the inheritance, and the idea made her weary just to think of it. By law, she was owed a portion of property to live upon. But to be forced out of her home, her sister's dowry taken . . . it was too much to think of. The weight of her troubles pressed down upon her, and Celeste pushed back the tears.

She couldn't weep. Tears would solve nothing at all. Instead, she reached for a cup of mead and drained it quickly, before accepting another. Without enough food in her stomach, the second drink made her light-headed. It didn't matter. She wanted to rid herself of the thoughts of failure.

She watched the other women, at the way they flirted. Without bothering to hide her interest, she rested her cheek against one hand and stared. No one had ever taught her how to attract a man's interest. When she had met Dougal at Locharr, he had made his interest known. He had come there to train with the baron's men, and she'd been fascinated by him from the first.

He'd found many reasons to be near her, until soon enough, they were stealing away to be alone. Just like the men and women here, though she and Dougal had never been lovers.

Celeste drank another glass of mead, watching as one woman caught a man's eye, smiled at him, and then went to speak to a different man.

Interesting. Was that what she should be doing? Instead of throwing herself at Dougal, should she be pursuing another man instead? Intrigued by the idea, she reached for a piece of mutton, nodding in welcome when Nairna sat down.

"Are you enjoying yourself, Lady Eiloch?"

"You may call me Celeste," she corrected. "And yes, I am. It was kind of you to host a gathering for me."

"Have you spoken with Dougal tonight?" Nairna asked.

Not since I kissed him, and he ordered me to stay away.

"A while ago, he showed me the horses." She toyed with her goblet.

Nairna sobered. "He spends far too much time with the animals. He needs a wife." Eyeing her closer, she added, "Have you considered him as a possibility?"

"I don't think Dougal has any interest in wedding a woman like me," Celeste said. She stood up and the ground seemed unsteady beneath her feet. "He'd prefer one of your maidens, I suppose."

"Then why is he staring at you?" Nairna countered, nodding toward the opposite side of the crowd. Celeste followed her gaze to where she saw Dougal holding his own cup of mead. Just as the woman had said, he was watching her.

"I don't know," she whispered. But his earlier kiss lingered with her still. She knew he'd done it to prove a point—that Edmon was nothing compared to him.

And she was well aware of it. She excused herself from Nairna, wanting to be alone. She skirted the crowd, moving closer to where a large bonfire blazed. Sparks drifted into the night sky, and several children danced while another clan member played the pipes.

"Will you dance with me?" came the voice of a young boy, perhaps seven years old. His brown hair was cut short, and he had a smile that could charm any girl into doing what he wanted. Celeste couldn't help but beam at him, and she took his hands. Several of the MacKinlochs were amused at the sight of them, but she was startled to find that the boy was quite good at dancing. He spun her around, and without meaning to, she started laughing. The mead, coupled with the dancing, made it nearly impossible to stand upright. But when she stumbled, another man caught her.

"Mind yourself, lass. We wouldna want you to be burned this night."

Celeste thanked him, but instead of giving her back to the boy, the man kept her hands in his. This time, the song had finished and another began that was slower. His palm rested upon her spine, and he added, "Kerr, I'll be dancing with the lady now. Find another and be off."

The boy looked disgruntled but did as he was ordered. Celeste stumbled again, but the man steadied her. "I am Robbie MacKinloch."

She ventured a smile, but the man's confidence made her feel uncertain. He was broad chested, with strong arms and a sword at his side. He, too, could be a protector. And yet . . . she found herself wishing she could hide away from all men. She went through the motions of dancing with Robbie, dimly aware of their conversation.

"Lady Eiloch?" He was waiting for an answer, and she realized she hadn't heard his question.

"I'm sorry. What was that?"

"I was asking if you'd like to walk with me by the loch."

Celeste glanced in the direction of the water, suddenly understanding that this man was offering exactly what she'd wanted—a private moment that could lead to more.

And yet, she found herself unable to move. Every instinct told her no. Why had she ever thought she could do this? The idea of lying beneath a stranger was appalling.

"Not just now," she said to him, apologizing as she excused herself. She kept walking through the crowds, past Dougal, until she stood near the stone wall surrounding the castle of Glen Arrin. Ivy had wound its way through the stones, covering the gray in a veil of green.

Footsteps sounded behind her, but she already knew who was following her now.

"I want her found," Lady Rowena demanded. Lionel de Laurent removed his helm, and his expression was shielded. "You know what will happen if she has conceived a child."

"I do."

His voice was like iron, and Rowena took comfort from it. Lionel was a strong man, a husband who would not allow anyone to threaten the future of their chilldren.

"I have sent a dozen men in search of her," he said quietly. "When the scouts return, we will bring her back, and that will be the end of it." His gray eyes sharpened. "If she were with child, she would not have fled."

"You don't know that. She might be trying to protect the babe."

Rowena would have done the same, were she in Celeste's place. She would do anything to guard her sons and daughter. Just as she would do whatever was necessary to secure their future inheritance.

She went to stand by the hearth in the solar, unable to stop herself from pacing. "There can be no child, Lionel."

"I know. But she has a strong reason to return. We hold her sister here." Although her husband's words were calm, Rowena took comfort in that. It was true that they could use Melisandre if necessary.

She smiled. "Perhaps we should send her a token to remind her of what she's left behind." A garment or perhaps Melisandre's long braid. "Something to lure her back."

Her husband did not smile. Instead, his gaze hardened. "We will find Celeste. Whether or not we bring her back alive depends upon her obedience."

Dougal followed Celeste beyond the crowd of people, deeper into the shadows. Although she likely knew he was there, she didn't speak. Only when he came to stand at her side did she admit, "Don't do this to me, Dougal. I don't want to be your enemy anymore."

She turned to face him, and the look of anguish in her eyes was a blow to his gut. "I can't go back and change the decisions I made. But it hurts me even more to see how much you've come to hate me."

"I don't hate you," he said quietly. "But I wish you hadn't returned."

"They don't know about me, do they?" She gripped her arms, the sadness evident. "You never told them."

"There was no reason to." He was glad he hadn't. At least then he could maintain his pride. "And if you say anything, I'll deny it."

Her face grew pensive. "I had my reasons for the choice I made. And I don't regret marrying Edmon. I only regret hurting you."

It wasn't the answer he wanted to hear. He'd wanted her to say that she'd made a terrible mistake, that she'd wanted to wed him. Not a Norman lord who'd given her silks and hundreds of acres.

"I suppose it was good that we didn't wed. For I now know that gold was more important to you than anything else."

She looked stricken at his words, and they'd hurt her the way he'd wanted them to. But to her credit, she made no denial.

"I never forgot you. Not then, and not now." She squared her shoulders and faced him. "I want you to go back with me. Be my escort and help me protect my sister. Melisandre is their hostage now."

He dug a little deeper for more information. "Have you no one else to help? Uncles or cousins?"

"My uncles live far to the south. Even if we did journey there, we might not find them. They're mercenary knights." She finally turned back to him. "I need a way of protecting her and—"

From the bleak expression on her face, he could see the dark fears. "I don't want to give up on Eiloch," she said. "Part of it is mine, by law. I want to fight for it. And you will have your reward if you come with me."

If he traveled with her to Eiloch, every hour would be nothing short of torment. Even now, Celeste's beauty was a siren's call, tempting him to cast aside common sense and accompany her on this futile quest.

God help him, no. He would not let her talk him into this. He'd kissed her because he wanted to punish her for choosing another man. To show her what it would have been like, had she wed him. Instead, it had only fired up the dormant feelings of desire.

"Please," she whispered. Without waiting for his refusal, she brushed past him, and her scent invaded his mind. Reminding him of the way she'd kissed him back, clinging to him.

Dougal waited for several minutes before returning to the bonfire. The contests had begun, and he saw other men lining up across from one another, bare-chested. The MacKinlochs enjoyed challenging one another in physical sparring, and his brothers were among those who fought.

"I've been wanting the chance to fight you again, Dougal," came the voice of Robbie. The man had removed his tunic and wore only trews. He had already defeated several men in wrestling, and his gaze narrowed upon Dougal.

This was not about physical prowess. In Robbie's eyes, Dougal had caught a hint of jealousy. He wanted to unman Dougal before the others, to prove himself a better protector for Celeste.

It wouldn't happen. Dougal had nothing to prove, for all the MacKinlochs had seen him defeat Robbie with no weapons, save his hands and his agility.

"I've bested you already," he told Robbie. "I've no need to do it again." The laughter and murmurs of approval surrounded him, as he crossed to stand by his brothers.

"Are you afraid you can't manage it a second time?" Robbie flexed his muscles, showing off his arms as he walked around the fire.

"No. I've simply no desire to humiliate you before the women."

It was the truth, but Robbie viewed the words as a taunt. "Come and fight, MacKinloch," he dared, beckoning.

Celeste didn't want either of them to fight, for she sensed that she would somehow end up caught in the middle. She had already made her decision and had no intention of letting the outcome be decided by a sparring match.

She wanted Dougal to be her champion. Not only because he was a strong man, easily able to guard her . . . but also because she wanted to heal the enmity between them.

"Don't fight over me," she asked, standing between the men. "Please."

"I would be glad to serve you," Robbie said. His gaze turned heated and he added, "In any way you would have me."

There were suggestive comments uttered by the crowd and a few whistles. His offer embarrassed her, though it was made in teasing. It was what she'd set out to do . . . find a man who would defend her, claim her and give her the bairn she needed. Undoubtedly, Robbie MacKinloch would do anything she asked. Yet, she couldn't allow that to happen. It was wrong.

She met his gaze for a moment, then turned back to look at Dougal. He'd stepped away, as if he'd predicted her decision and didn't care what she did. When she studied his face, it was devoid of all emotion. If she walked away with Robbie this very moment, Dougal would do nothing to stop her.

But she didn't want Robbie. She wanted the man whose kiss had shaken her out of slumber into a moment where her world was made real again. Where she no longer felt so desperately alone.

"You are a brave fighter," she said to Robbie after a long pause, "and I am grateful to you for the offer." She squared her shoulders, facing the crowd. "But I have already asked Dougal MacKinloch to be my guard."

The color in Robbie's face darkened. She tried not to look at him but instead stared at Dougal. His brown eyes had narrowed, his mouth taut with banked fury.

He didn't want this at all—she understood that. But she'd put him in a position where he could say nothing to deny her without doing so in front of everyone.

She moved through the people, seeking her own retreat, but Dougal was pushing his way past his brother's wife, heading straight toward her.

To her shock, he spoke loud enough for others to hear. "Robbie is a skilled fighter. And he would still go in my place if you asked it of him."

He was telling her no, admitting his reluctance before everyone. It would only be right to accept his reasons and let him go. But she was not willing to give up just yet. Instead, she continued her retreat, moving far away from the others so that no one would overhear them.

"I have not asked it of him," she responded quietly. "I've asked it of you."

A dark rage slid across Dougal's face. "You do not command me," he said, his voice like the edge of a blade. "You do not come into my home and make demands."

"I asked for help—"

"There was no asking." He moved forward and gripped her around the waist. All of a sudden, her decision no longer seemed like a sound one. She hadn't considered his response would be this angry.

"Where are you taking me? I'm not going anywhere." She twisted against him, but he countered by lifting her up. She tried to fight his grasp, but his strength far overpowered hers.

"I'm taking you somewhere we can talk without a thousand ears listening." He strode farther away from the others, her waist tight in his grasp.

She went motionless, realizing what this could mean. He took her outside the gates and toward the dozens of small crofters' homes, with thatched roofs and walls made of mud. A dark memory assailed her, of living in a house hardly fit for pigs, much less her mother and siblings.

He led her into a home so small, she could cross the room in three strides. A small pallet lay on one end, and the peat fire had died down to coals.

Calm yourself, she ordered. *He only wants to talk.*

"This is where you live?" she asked.

He nodded. "I built this place with my own hands. It's enough for me." Crossing his arms over his chest, he added, "Though I suppose you would look down on it."

She moved to the far wall, touching the wattle-and-daub walls. He made it sound as if she valued wealth over love. And years ago, his accusation might have held a grain of truth. But, at the time, she'd not been thinking clearly. She and her sister were starving, and when she'd had a choice between giving Melisandre a home and everything she'd ever wanted, it had felt selfish to choose Dougal. She didn't deserve love—not when it meant an uncertain future for her sister.

And so, she'd made an unforgiveable decision.

"There's nothing wrong with your home," she said softly.

"It wasn't good enough for you when I asked you to marry me two years ago." His words lashed at her, breaking down her emotions. "You chose a man you hardly knew because he owned hundreds of acres."

Her hands curled against the wood, and she didn't bother to hide her tears. "You meant everything to me."

"If I meant so much to you, then why did you choose another man to wed?" The words were so quiet, they held a razor's edge.

"Because I was afraid." Seeing this place only brought back all the harsh memories of her childhood. She remembered the hunger in her sister's face and the cold body of her infant brother. Living in this way would mean returning to those terrifying days of not knowing whether they had enough food to survive the winter.

"Afraid of what?"

She didn't know how to tell him the truth. None of the words would win his forgiveness, no matter what she said. Dougal was a man of action, not words.

Instead, she chose a place to sit, resting her hand against her cheek. He waited endless moments for her to explain. But the more time stretched between them, the harsher the knots in her stomach grew.

"You had no right to demand that I be your protector," he began. "In front of my family and kin, no less."

"You're the one I trust the most. And as I told you before, I'll reward you for your time." She went to add peat to the fire, feeling suddenly nervous about his proximity. Not to mention the anger she'd aroused in him.

"I want nothing from you, Celeste," he said. "Except for you to leave."

Her skin tightened at his words, and she turned back to him. "If you wanted me to leave, then why did you bring me here?"

He had no answer for that. In the darkness between them, she waited to see what he would do. Her heart began beating faster as he stood on the far side of the hut.

Hot-tempered, Dougal was not a man who would be manipulated by anyone, though that was not her intention. The air between them was heated with anger and something indefinable. Something that made her blood race against her skin. She took a tentative step forward, sensing that there was far more that he'd held back.

"Why, Dougal?"

Another step. She froze when he closed the distance. "Choose another protector, Lady Eiloch."

"Don't call me that again. My name is Celeste." Her voice came out in the barest whisper.

When he reached up to her face, her skin erupted in gooseflesh. Slowly, he grazed her cheek with his knuckles, until his hand came beneath her chin. "I don't know what it is you want . . . Celeste." He breathed her name as if it were a curse. "But I'll not let you use me again. If it's a hired sword you want, then find someone else."

She pressed his hand away, shocked at how hot his skin was. Though she only grazed the edge of his palm, in her mind the vision spun of his rough palms upon her bare flesh. Of what it would be like to lie beneath a man such as this.

"And if it's not a hired sword I want?" she whispered, wondering what had possessed her to be so daring.

He moved in so fast, she had no time to realize what she'd done. Her back was pressed to the wall, his hard body against hers.

If she continued to push him, she would get what she wanted. But it would not be a calm night of surrender. This man would claim her body, ravaging her with his mouth and hands.

The very thought made her go liquid inside, her body rising to his.

"Will you guard me?" she asked. "Just for a little while?" Against her hips, she felt his hard erection, and the firm pressure kindled her own desire to be taken.

"And who will keep you safe from me?" he demanded. His dark eyes stared into hers before he stepped back and guided her toward the door. "Go back to the castle. Before I take something you're not offering."

Chapter Four

Dougal didn't sleep that night. His body ached for a release only she could grant him. Inwardly, he damned Celeste for coming here. Never before had any woman tempted him this much. He wanted to take her, to spend the night exploring her delicate skin while her hair fell down to her hips.

God above, she tempted him. But he would never lower his pride to ask. He'd seen the look of dismay on her face when she'd viewed his simple home. She didn't want a man like him, who had only a tiny plot of land and a thatched hut to call his own. His only valued possession was the mare, and he spent more time with Ivory than his own family.

She was far above him, like a princess . . . and he was the lowly servant. Perhaps that was what she wanted. A man to serve her.

He was no woman's slave. Never would be.

His hands dug into the sleeping pallet, and he rolled onto his stomach, trying to suppress the painful aching in his groin. He would tell Celeste no and find someone else to escort her from Glen Arrin. And when he did, his brothers' wives would berate him for it. He'd never hear an end to their chattering, for they believed that a man was only happy when he had a wife.

He wouldn't argue that he'd be glad of a wife at this moment, someone to ease the sexual frustration in him. Although he'd had a few women over the years, he'd done his best to avoid them, ever since Celeste had gone.

It was nearly dawn, and he rose and dressed. Outside, the spring air held a chill, and he rubbed his hands together for warmth. The gray sky held streaks of rose, and he walked silently toward the stables.

Ivory was waiting for him, and he fed her and walked with her in circles, praising her when she obeyed. Today, he intended to try placing a saddle on her back, and he waited until she was calm before attempting it. Though she didn't like the weight, he rewarded her when she remained steady, allowing him to secure it.

"Good morn to you," came the voice of Laren MacKinloch. Dougal glanced over and Laren held out a bundle of food. "I thought you might be hungry."

He kept his grip on the lead and brought the mare over as he greeted his brother's wife. She gave him leftover food from the feasting last night, cold mutton and oat cakes. The repast was welcome, but he knew she was here to convince him to go with Lady Eiloch.

When she continued to remain silent, he handed her back the bundle and asked, "Well? Aren't you going to convince me that I'll dishonor the MacKinloch name if I don't go with her?"

To his surprise, she shook her head. "I came to ask what *you* wanted. If you want me to find someone else to escort her, I will. Despite last night, Robbie would do it."

He caught himself before he uttered a retort. The idea of Robbie escorting Celeste anywhere made him uneasy. The man would take advantage of her at the first opportunity.

"What do you want, Dougal?" she repeated.

"I want to be left alone," he said, reaching up to touch the mare's cheek. "I don't want any part of her battle."

She inclined her head. "Then I will see to it that she leaves." Pausing a moment, she added, "But when she returned from your hut last night, she was crying."

Resentment edged his temper at the suggestion that he'd caused her tears. "I did nothing to her."

Laren gave a sympathetic smile, "I know that, Dougal." Her eyes softened as she continued, "But I saw the way she was watching you. And I know that you asked her to wed you two years ago."

He couldn't hide his surprise. "How did you find that out?"

She sent him a secretive smile, ignoring his question. "She came back for a reason." Laren reached out to pat the mare. "And I think it's because she loves you still."

Her gaze turned searching, but he shook his head. "She wants me as a guard, nothing more."

Laren eyed him with concern. "You are my brother by marriage, and you deserve more than a life with these horses."

"Let it be, Laren," he said. "I enjoy my life the way it is."

She nodded. "So be it. But I thought you'd want to know that she's leaving now. There are men lined up, wanting to be her escort." With a nod to him, she walked back in the direction she'd come.

A line of men. It didn't surprise him, not with Celeste's beauty. She had a face men would die for and a body that had kept him awake all night long.

Dougal grimaced, remembering the softness of her mouth against his. He wanted to spend a night losing himself in that sensual mouth, learning every inch of her slender body. But those thoughts were dangerous.

Dougal ran his hands over Ivory's back and swung up into the saddle. He needed to clear his head and exercise the mare.

He rode past the gates, keeping Ivory in a controlled canter. The ground was uneven, and he wanted her to have a sure footing. As he let her go, his mind blurred with the question of what Celeste wanted from him. She'd said she didn't want to be his enemy.

He didn't want to be friends, either. Beneath the anger of the past two years was the desire to prove himself to her. To make her regret her choices.

When he reached the edge of the MacKinloch lands, smoke rose from a distant fire. A few tents were set up, and he pulled the mare to a stop, wondering who was there. One man emerged from his tent, and Dougal spied the glint of chainmail armor.

Though it might be only English troops, it was too small a group for an invasion. More likely, they had come for Lady Eiloch.

The safest thing to do was to put his family first, letting her go. And yet, the thought of surrendering her to these men was impossible. Celeste had put her trust in him, wanting him to keep her safe. Though he might not want to be involved, neither did he want to see her harmed. Her blue eyes haunted him, and her kiss had awakened a temptation that simmered beneath his skin.

Damn her for it.

Dougal turned Ivory back, urging her toward their fortress. As the horse picked up speed, he considered what to do. Giving Celeste back to the soldiers wasn't safe. She'd fled Eiloch, and if they'd sent armed men after her, their intent was not friendly. He didn't even know if they would keep her alive.

But the last thing he wanted was to bring this battle into Glen Arrin, where his friends and family might be harmed. Although she was safe here, it might be better to lead them away. Perhaps toward Locharr or Cairnross.

He rode through the gates, already knowing what he must do. Celeste was waiting on the far side of the fortress, already mounted on her horse while Nairna finished giving her more supplies. Half a dozen men stood at the ready, while her gaze scanned each of them. The men waiting were all unmarried, some barely into adulthood, while other, older men had been widowed. Every last one of them was staring at Lady Eiloch as if he wanted to share her bed. And she, in turn, looked uncomfortable at the prospect.

When Nairna caught sight of him, she sent him a chiding glare. Dougal ignored her and rode forward until he reached the front of the crowd. Celeste's face relaxed visibly, as if she'd been hoping he would change his mind.

When one of the men ventured too close, Ivory whinnied, rearing up, and Dougal had to hold fast to keep from being thrown off. He spoke to the mare lightly, nudging her with his knees to bring her away from all the people. Only after he'd calmed her did he look back at Celeste.

"The soldiers from Eiloch are just beyond the hill," he said. "And if you don't want to be caught, you should come with me now."

Celeste had no idea where Dougal was guiding them, but he kept up a relentless pace. They left Glen Arrin through a hidden gate near the back of the fortress, but it wasn't long before she spied Lionel de Laurent and his men in pursuit.

Her heartbeat quickened, and she leaned forward against her horse, praying Dougal could get her to safety. She hardly cared where they went, so long as it wasn't back to Eiloch.

Her horse could not keep up with his mare, who was breaking hard through the meadow. She'd never seen any animal move with such speed. When she glanced behind, Lord Eiloch's men were gaining on them. Though Celeste urged her horse faster, she feared there was little hope of losing her pursuers.

"Dougal!" she shouted to him, needing him to come closer. He slowed the mare for a moment, and without warning, her horse reared up, screaming in pain. Three arrows were embedded in the horse's side, one in its neck.

Saints have mercy, she prayed. If they were shooting at her, then they meant to kill her.

Dougal rode in fast, seizing her from the saddle before she could fall. With his arms around her waist, he pulled her onto his own horse, urging the mare faster. The speed was terrifying, but she marveled that the animal could carry her weight and keep up such a pace.

"They want you dead, don't they?" Dougal said against her ear. "They don't plan to take you captive."

She didn't answer, her mind frozen at the thought. Closing her eyes tightly, she wondered if there was any escape at all. Or if she would live through this day.

"I'm sorry," she whispered at last. Likely he didn't hear her against the thunder of the mare's pace, but his arm tightened imperceptibly around her waist.

After a time, Lord Eiloch's men faded into the distance. Dougal changed their direction at one interval, veering off the main road and taking them deeper into the mountains. The shadowed hills were blanketed with green, the morning mist obscuring the forest. He deliberately led them into the heart of the clouded mountains, through groves of fir trees. With the slower pace, Celeste grew more aware of his arms around her and the hard-muscled thighs pressed against her backside.

She did not speak, not daring to break the stillness. Instead, she drank in the beauty of the misted mountains, riding countless miles along a worn path in the trees. Once, they stopped to let the mare drink, but even then, Dougal maintained his silence.

After so many hours, she was beginning to wonder if he ever intended to tell her their destination. They had traveled far past Locharr, and it was now late afternoon. She'd had nothing to eat at all, and her stomach was gnawing itself with hunger. Finally, she could stand it no longer.

As he led her through another valley, she stopped to ask, "Where are you taking me, Dougal?"

"We'll visit my brother Callum and his wife at Cairnross. Their fortress is a day's journey away, and we'll reach it by tomorrow night."

Tomorrow night? She hadn't anticipated it would take that long.

"Will the soldiers catch up to us?" Although they had managed to escape Lionel's forces for now, she didn't know whether the men could track them here.

Dougal shook his head. "Not this night." He guided her toward a hidden pathway that led up a steep incline. "We're a few hours ahead of them now, and it's too dark for them to find us." He pointed toward a small pool of water in a small clearing and added, "We'll make camp here."

That much was a relief. He helped her dismount and removed the saddle and blanket from the mare, rubbing her down after the ride. Celeste suddenly realized that when the men had shot her horse, they'd lost all their supplies. Dismayed, she went to get a drink from the pond, but the hunger was making her light-headed. "Is there anything to eat?" she asked him.

Dougal withdrew some strips of dried meat from a pouch at his side. "Take these. And I'll hunt for our dinner while you start a fire." He gave her flint, and she set it aside while she gathered tinder and wood.

He was gone for a long time. Celeste built a fire and sat beside it, trying to warm herself. Yet, it did nothing at all to dispel her fear. Lord Eiloch's men weren't going to let her live. They would hunt her down, and her death meant they would inherit all of Edmon's lands. Melisandre would be sent away to fend for herself.

Her hands began shaking, though she tried to push back the fear. She hadn't known, until now, how much danger she was in. She could not go back.

And yet, she *must* go back. Her sister's life depended on it.

Dougal returned within the hour with two ducks. While he prepared them to roast, she gathered several stout branches and propped them against a wide tree, creating a small shelter. Using the blanket from Ivory's back, she covered the lean-to and then unfastened her cloak to cover the cold ground.

Dougal eyed her creation and nodded with approval. "That will do well for the night." He set up the water fowl to roast and then came to sit beside her. Celeste was aware of his proximity, and she spoke at last.

"Thank you for helping me escape them," she said, easing to her knees. He was staring at the fire, and though he gave a nod, there was tension in his posture. He looked uneasy, and his hand kept slipping to the dirk at his side as if ensuring it was still there.

"Dougal," she said softly, "I am sorry for what happened between us. I was hoping . . . we could be friends again."

He said nothing, but kept his gaze fixated upon the flames. His lack of an answer discomfited her. Was it so hard to be friends? Her earlier fear was replaced by annoyance. To get his attention, she picked a handful of grass and tossed it at him. "Didn't you hear what I said?"

He stared down at the grass sprinkled over his trews. "You threw grass at me?" The disbelief on his face was almost laughable.

"I didn't think you'd want me to throw rocks." She pulled another handful in an invisible threat. "It's not the first time I threw something at you. Remember the leaves that day when we were in the woods?" It had begun when she'd made an enormous pile of autumn leaves, tossing them in the air.

"I remember what happened after our leaf battle," he said.

Her smile faded. He'd pressed her back into the leaf pile, his body on top of hers while he'd kissed her senseless. From the feral look in his eyes, he wasn't thinking about leaves at all.

"I think you've forgotten how to have fun, Dougal," she remarked, flinging the handful of grass on his shoulder. "Or how to smile."

She tiptoed away from him, slipping into the darkening woods. Hiding behind one of the trees, she waited for him to come and find her. When he didn't move, she chose a tree with low branches and climbed onto one of them.

"I don't want to play, Celeste."

She held her silence, wondering if he would pursue her. It had been a way of teasing one another years ago. When he'd found her, he'd stolen a kiss as his prize. And when she'd found him, she'd done the same.

The limb was cool and hard against her back. From her vantage point, she could see him by the fire while the ducks cooked. He picked up a branch and tossed it on the flames before he stood at last, staring out into the darkness.

"You're behaving like a child," he called out, walking toward her.

Maybe she was, but if she could pull him out of this dark mood, it was worth it. She didn't want to dwell upon the past years of hurt and heartbreak. For tonight, she wanted to remember the way they'd laughed together.

"And your hiding places were never very good," he remarked, crossing his arms as he stared up at her in the tree.

"I never tried to hide very well," she admitted. "I wanted you to find me."

He let out a sigh, and she picked a leaf, dropping it down to him. "Let the past go, Dougal. Let us just be friends, as we were."

He climbed up to her and moved to sit upon the branch beside her. "Is that what you want?" He picked a leaf and drew it over her cheek. The cool green texture was soft, and the touch slid over her in a caress. He let the leaf fall, and her defenses drifted away with it.

No, she didn't want to be merely friends. He had a way of seeing through her, to the heart of what she wanted. There was a desperate urge to feel his mouth upon hers, the wild hunger that only he could evoke.

"I didn't mean to draw you into such danger," she said, leaning a little closer. "I never thought they would try to kill me."

His dark eyes regarded her with a steady intent. "I won't allow anyone to harm you."

The warmth of his voice entranced her, and she closed her eyes, wishing he could protect her from the world. Despite the cool air, she felt perfectly warm, so close to him. Safe, even.

"You found me, Dougal," she breathed. "Will you not claim your prize?"

From the way he stared at her, a warmth rose within her skin. In his eyes, she saw the memory of the kiss they'd shared and the shielded desire. Would he take what she was offering?

Abruptly, his expression shifted. "No, Celeste. Not this time." His words were meant to sever any feelings, cutting all invisible ties between them.

It might have worked, had she not seen the haunted look in his eyes.

Dougal climbed down from the tree, then lifted her to the ground. He returned to the fire and removed the roasted ducks, handing her one of them. She propped up the wooden stake, allowing the meat to cool first. Nothing had ever tasted so good as that first bite. She ate quickly, never minding how hot it was.

Dougal tore through his own meat, and after a moment, she dared to smile again. "Look at us. We're like barbarians who haven't eaten in weeks."

He wiped his hands but didn't return the smile. They ate without speaking, and after a while, he finally voiced the question. "You said you wouldn't wed me because you were afraid. I want to know why."

She avoided an answer at first, wondering if she dared to give him the reasons. He might not understand.

Staring down at the bones of the duck, she admitted, "I was often hungry when I was a girl. I learned to enjoy a good meal when it was offered to me." She wiped her hands and forced herself to look at him. "Did you know why I came to Locharr?"

"I assumed you were being fostered there."

She shook her head. "Melisandre and I asked the baron for sanctuary after our father and mother died."

He asked no questions, but waited for her to continue. She gripped her hands around her knees, feeling the chill of the night.

"All my life, my father spent his coins on useless things. Sometimes a length of silk for a gown or a silver cup for my mother. He thought the gifts would please us, but then there was no money left for food." She didn't look up at Dougal, unsure of what he would think. "He went into debt, and we were the ones who paid the price. My mother would try to sell the goods, but there are not many folk who will buy silk during a harsh winter."

"How did he die?"

She tightened her knuckles, trying to stop herself from shaking. "He bought several flasks of wine and drank them all. We tried to awaken him, but he was already dead."

She sobered and faced Dougal, admitting, "Not long after that my mother lost her milk. My baby brother died of starvation, and she took her own life in grief."

The trembling took her and the heaviness of loss shadowed her again. "I had to take care of my sister, and that's when I brought her to Locharr. I told the baron everything, and he promised to seek a good marriage for me. I vowed I would never live like that again."

The dark fear of poverty would never leave her. It went bone deep, and he needed to know that. She drew her knees up beneath her gown. "Then I met you."

She reached out a hand to him, wondering if he would understand what she needed from him. But he didn't take it.

"You thought I was the same as your father."

"No, that wasn't the reason. I was afraid. The baron gave us a place to stay when we'd lost all our belongings. After the trouble he went to, finding a good match for me . . . it wasn't possible to say no. Regardless of how I felt about you."

She let him see her tears, baring her fears and lost dreams before him. "I hated myself for refusing you. But I had no right to choose my heart's desire. Not when I had to provide for my sister."

"You should have trusted me," he argued.

She shook her head. "You don't know what it's like, Dougal. To go hungry, wondering if you'll ever eat again. To watch your family starve before your eyes."

"You're wrong." He stood, his mood growing darker. "When I was twelve, I had to steal food from the kitchens when they forgot about me."

She said nothing, but this was a side to him she hadn't known about.

"My mother was too busy to worry about me. My father was dead and my brothers were prisoners. It was up to her to lead the defense of the fortress, and she grew tired of the fighting. She left me when I was fourteen. I know how it feels to be left behind. To not know if anyone will take care of you."

She stood up and walked toward him. He kept his back to her, but she didn't want him to push her away. Not now.

Instead, she stood behind him and reached for his hand. This time, he didn't pull away when she squeezed it in silent understanding. Right now, she wanted to lean against him once more, to feel his strong arms around her. To pretend for a moment that he would guard her from any foe. Especially those that haunted her from the past.

"I'm sorry," she whispered, resting her cheek against his back. He didn't move away, which offered a fragile hope.

"What do you want from me, Celeste? Am I to help you steal your sister away and bring you both to safety?"

She could not tell him the truth, that she had originally hoped to conceive a child and remain at Eiloch. Now that she realized it was such a foolish idea, she had discarded it entirely. "I don't know the answers, Dougal. But I cannot live in peace with the new Lord Eiloch and his wife ."

"They want you to die."

"I think so, yes. And my sister is still there." She couldn't suppress a shudder, feeling utterly helpless.

He said nothing for a long time, the fire being the only crackling noise to break the stillness. "Go to the shelter," he said at last. "Sleep, and I'll think of what we can do."

She took his other hand in hers. "There is space enough for both of us."

Tonight was the first time they'd taken a step toward forgiveness. It seemed that he was now willing to help her, that perhaps he saw the reasons behind the choices she'd made.

She wanted to lie beside him tonight, to feel the warmth of his body close. And if Dougal were to join her within the space, she could not deny what might happen between them.

But as she lay down within the small shelter, he continued to sit by the fire, remaining far away from her.

The temptation beckoned to him, to enter the shelter and share the space. But after Celeste's confession, he needed time to reconsider everything. She'd come back to him, seeking help. And though he might want to deny it, the old feelings were still there, buried beneath the years of separation.

She *had* cared for him, even though she'd wed Lord Eiloch. He sensed that it had been a painful decision, one she hadn't wanted to make. But it infuriated him that she hadn't even been willing to try. She'd judged him based on the poverty she saw and had decided he could offer her no future.

It pricked him like a thorn digging into his pride. *You weren't good enough for her,* came the voice of reason.

But she'd made the choice out of fear. Not because she hadn't cared. And that changed the face of his anger.

Celeste was watching him from within the primitive shelter, resting her face upon one hand. "Are you going to sit out there and freeze all night?"

"It's nearly summer." But she was right; the nights were cold. Given the choice, he would be far more comfortable within the shelter she'd built. Her body heat would be more than enough to warm him. Yet, he doubted if he could sleep beside her without touching her.

"I've already told you, there's no reason to be afraid of sharing the shelter. We'll both sleep easier." She ventured a light smile, as if she had no idea what she was proposing.

Dougal didn't trust himself. He was weary from last night's frustration and another day of traveling. "Neither of us would get any sleep at all," he predicted.

"You might be right." She crept out of the tent, still kneeling on the ground. "Edmon used to accuse me of stealing the coverlet. Often I would roll up in it, leaving him with naught."

The memory made her face soften, but it had a very different effect upon him. Jealousy roared through him, at the thought of her lying with another man. He imagined Celeste naked, wearing nothing except a coverlet. "If you'd been my wife, I'd have stolen it back."

"You'd have to fight me for it," she teased, her eyes bright. "I like to be kept warm at night."

Oh, he'd have kept her warm all right. His groin tightened at the thought.

Around her neck, Celeste still wore the glass pendant Nairna had loaned her. It had slipped beneath the neckline of her gown, between her breasts. His attention rested upon her, and he wondered why she persisted in asking him to join her.

Her hair was still undone from the night before, a curled lock sliding over one shoulder. Strands of molten gold mingled with darker brown hair.

"Did you love him?" he demanded, even though he didn't want to know the true answer.

"He was good to me. And we were friends."

And there was the unspoken answer. No, she hadn't loved Lord Eiloch. A primitive side to his mood was satisfied to hear it, for he wanted to know that her heart belonged to him.

The way she was watching him now made his body respond in ways he didn't want it to. "Go back to the tent without me," he ordered.

"But—"

"Now. Or you'll find yourself on your back and I'll be touching you in ways your husband never did."

She stood with her mouth parted, shocked at his words. For a moment, she didn't move, as if questioning whether he was serious. To underscore his words, Dougal moved in and touched the shoulders of her gown. "Right now, I'm wanting to slide this off your skin." He loosened the laces, watching her flush as he did just that. When her shoulder was bared, he brought his mouth to her bare flesh. He nipped at it, meaning to frighten her.

"If you invite me into that shelter, I'll take this gown off you, and use my mouth upon every part of your body." He kissed her throat, feeling the tension in her. "Don't fool yourself into believing I have honor. If you invite me back, I'll take what you're offering. And far more than you want to give."

Her heart was slamming against her ribs as Celeste retreated into the shelter. His words had taken apart her courage, reminding her of exactly what happened between a man and a woman. And although she'd accepted her husband's lovemaking, it had never been anything but lying there and enduring his attention. It had done nothing to arouse her.

But Dougal's threats had slid beneath her skin, awakening her in a way she didn't understand. Between her legs she was wet and aching. And although this was what she'd wanted, she found herself unable to speak the words of invitation. In the end, she was a coward, afraid of the way he made her feel.

She didn't recognize this woman she was transforming into. And instinctively she knew, at the very deepest level, that it would be impossible to lie with a man like Dougal and walk away. It would change her.

For beneath it all, she hadn't forgotten the way he made her feel. He'd stolen her heart once before. And now, he'd warned her that if she dared to pursue this, he wouldn't stop.

God help her, she didn't want him to.

Her gown was bunched between her legs, and the pressure was a sweet torment. Her breathing had gone faster, and in the darkness she watched him. He was sharpening one of his blades upon a stone, seated on a log as he worked. His dark hair hung below his shoulders, his eyes intent upon his task.

As his hands moved, she tightened her legs together, and something began to quicken inside her. The sweet pressure was rising, and she reached up to touch one of her breasts. The sensation sent the echo of desire between her legs, and she tried to remember what it had been like to have her husband inside her.

Except it was Dougal she imagined now. She closed her eyes, wondering what it would feel like to have this man penetrating her, his hard length filling her deeply. She could hardly breathe, hardly think. The feeling swelled inside, and she brought her hand beneath her skirts, startled at how wet the thoughts had made her. The release came so fast, she arched against her own hand, her body shuddering.

And when it was over, she felt ashamed at herself. She was throwing herself at him, knowing that they still could not be together. It was wrong, and if he knew why she had come to him, he'd never forgive her.

In the darkness, she closed her eyes, wondering how she would ever unravel herself from this knotted fate.

CHAPTER FIVE

"Dougal!" Lady Marguerite hurried forward to greet them. "What a wonderful surprise!" A genuine smile spread over the woman's face. She had married his brother Callum years ago, and Dougal still viewed her as an angel. After Callum had been freed from prison, he'd lost his voice. Only Marguerite had been able to bring him back out of the years of torture.

Within moments, his brother appeared, holding the hand of his eldest son, Ailric. The lad gripped a bow in his hand, and at the sight of the boy, Dougal smiled. He'd carved that bow himself, out of an ash tree. The boy had spent three years at Glen Arrin but visited his parents often. Marguerite had insisted that she did not want her children forgetting who their mother and father were during their fostering.

Dougal helped Celeste dismount and led her forward. "This is Celeste de Laurent, Lady of Eiloch. Her escorts were killed on her way to Glen Arrin. I've promised her my protection until she can return to her sister."

Celeste greeted Marguerite, and while the two women spoke, his older brother sent him a silent question. Dougal didn't know how to answer for he hadn't decided what would become of them. Celeste's revelation had explained a great deal about why she'd refused to wed him, though he wished she'd given him the truth long ago.

She hadn't trusted him to take care of her then. But would she trust him now? Did he want her to stay? His thoughts stood upon shifting ground, for he didn't have the answers. For now, he would keep her safe. Beyond that, he didn't know.

"Eiloch is a long way from here," Marguerite was saying. "Come and refresh yourselves. I'll see to it that you have food and drink." She smiled warmly and gave orders to a servant while Callum led them inside.

The fortress had changed a great deal, having been rebuilt from the ground up. Although Cairnross was not large, the stone walls were thick, lending a good deal of protection. The main house was made of wood, and the comforting smell of a peat fire lingered in the air.

A three-year-old girl ran over to Callum and grabbed his knees. "Hello, my lass," he greeted her. He swung Nicole into the air, and the girl squealed with delight, chattering to her father and laughing. Then she nestled against him, staring at Dougal.

"She adores her father," Marguerite said, bemused by the pair. "He gives her anything she wants."

An unexpected vision ripped through Dougal, of a daughter with Celeste's blue eyes. From the wistful look on her face, he could see that she did long to be a mother. Perhaps it was wrong of him, but he was glad that Edmon de Laurent had never given her a child.

"Have some wine, and we'll talk," Callum offered, leading them inside to sit down. But his brother's expression held wariness. While Marguerite poured them cups of wine, he added, "My men saw a dozen soldiers approaching from the west. Searching for her, I suspect."

"Aye." Dougal noticed the way his brother held his daughter tighter, in a silent reminder that he would protect his children and his wife. "But you have archers. They won't get close."

"But more men will come," his brother predicted. "Why do they want her?"

"They want my widow's portion," Celeste answered. "If I am dead, then they inherit everything."

"How long until they arrive?" Dougal asked.

"A few hours," Callum answered. "Maybe less." He took a sip from his own goblet, setting his daughter down and sending her off to play. "You should keep Lady Eiloch hidden when they arrive. We'll let them search here, to avoid suspicion. When they are satisfied that she's gone, they'll leave and continue searching. We'll take them along a different path."

Celeste paled at his words. "I didn't realize they had caught up to us." She pushed her own goblet away, looking up at Dougal with fear. "I don't want to bring enemies among you. That was never my intent." Taking a deep breath, she added, "Perhaps we should go now, before they arrive."

"No, my brother is right. If we run, we'll be seen." Dougal took her hand, wanting to reassure her. Callum would not have suggested hiding her if he did not have a place where she could not be found. "We'll leave in the middle of the night when they cannot track us."

Celeste squeezed his fingers, but he didn't miss the fear.

"There's a hidden chamber belowground, for storage," Marguerite said. "Lord Cairnross used to keep prisoners there years ago. No one will find you . . . but I fear it's very cold."

Celeste looked at him, and though she tried to put on a brave face, he saw her fear of being alone.

"It will be all right," he reassured her. "I'll stay with you."

She took a deep breath and ventured, "What about our tracks? They won't believe we're gone if the tracks end here."

He let out a slow breath, understanding what she wanted him to do.

"Take Ivory and lead them deeper into the hills," she continued. "I'll . . . stay belowground in hiding as long as I must." She squared her shoulders, her face appearing calm.

But he saw the truth in her eyes. She had reason to fear, for they had already fired arrows at her. If a single soldier found her, she might die.

"She's right," Callum agreed. "They've already tracked you this far."

Dougal stared at Celeste, wondering if he dared to leave her behind. Though she nodded, he didn't miss the slight tremble at her lips. There was nothing he could do to ease her fear.

Callum reached for his bow, leaning down to kiss his wife. "We won't be gone long. Hide her until our return." Marguerite nodded and touched his face, her hands lingering upon his cheek.

Color rose in Celeste's face. She was trying to remain calm, but when she met Dougal's gaze, he saw the worry lurking.

"I'll return for you. I promise." He rested his hand upon her spine in reassurance.

Marguerite led them toward the back of the Hall, where she lifted an iron ring, revealing a ladder that led belowground. "It's down here," she said, picking up a torch from an iron sconce on one wall.

"You can go with your brother," Celeste told him. "I'll be fine." But even as she said the words, her eyes looked down into the darkness with undisguised fear.

"I won't be gone long," he promised. "We'll lead them to a false trail." But although she braved a smile, he saw through it. She took another breath to steady herself and then suddenly threw herself into his arms, gripping him hard.

He understood her need for comfort and security. The warmth of human touch soothed in a way words could not.

"Don't be hurt on my behalf. No matter what happens," she urged.

He kept his arms locked around her, breathing in the scent of her skin and marking a memory. The softness of her, the wordless gratitude, were so unexpected he couldn't speak a word. Instead, he let his touch speak for him, resting his face against her hair while both arms held her tight.

"I feel safe with you," she confessed. "And . . . I need you to return."

Her blue eyes revealed the uncertainty, and she reached up to touch his roughened cheek. Aye, he fully intended to return to this woman. Especially with the way she was looking at him now.

"Remain in hiding until I come for you," he commanded. Without knowing why, he leaned down and kissed her hard. She nodded, and when he left, he shielded the wayward thoughts and the empty ache that had begun inside him.

The chamber was so frigid, Celeste could see her breath against the lonely torch Marguerite had given her. The cold night was an enemy impossible to defeat, despite the fur she wrapped around herself. It was a fear that sank into her veins, reminding her of how alone she was.

She leaned against the wall, thinking of Dougal. He possessed a strength that made her want to lean upon him and take comfort. With each day she'd spent at his side, her feelings for him had only intensified.

She'd wed Edmon de Laurent to give Melisandre the life neither of them had before. Though it had broken her apart to leave Dougal, she'd believed it was wiser to follow the urging of her head rather than her heart. She'd sacrificed herself, leaving the man she loved...the man she had never stopped loving. She couldn't say what had rekindled the feelings, but time had not diminished them. She'd only pressed them deep inside, believing they would go away.

Beneath the fur coverlet Marguerite had given her, Celeste was trembling, though no longer from the cold. Dougal's kiss had twined around her fragile heart, tempting her to see the man he was and not the guardian he represented.

Was there anything left between them now? Or was he protecting her only for the gain it would bring him? He might not want her anymore . . . only a stallion for his beloved mare. Guarding her was a means to an end. Hadn't he pushed her aside time and again?

Let him go, her head insisted. *Find another way to protect Melisandre. A way that didn't involve risking her feelings.*

Celeste sensed that she was treading within shallow water that could drown her. It would take very little to push Dougal over the edge, to bring him into her bed. And after it was done, he might claim his own vengeance, leaving her behind.

Her earlier plan now seemed like the impulsive plan of a girl, not one that would offer any protection. Even if she did conceive a child, Rowena would never leave her in peace. The woman was ruthless and cared for nothing, save her own children. It was not safe to return. And it was not safe for Melisandre.

Dougal would keep his word to defend them both. But each moment she spent with him weakened the walls around her heart. He deserved better than a woman like her. She should let him go, ignoring the desire he'd conjured.

For if she did set aside her inhibitions, it would bare her heart in a way that would only break when they parted ways.

Dougal rode for an hour north while the soldiers searched Cairnross. Although Marguerite had promised that it was impossible for anyone to find Celeste, he couldn't let go of the sense that he should be there with her. Both of them knew what would happen if they caught her.

He gritted his teeth against the thought, turning back and retracing his path back toward the fortress. When he reached the river, he drew the mare into the water, hiding her tracks there. Again, he changed direction, leading Ivory into the hills, obscuring any tracks he'd made. He waited on higher ground until it was late afternoon. Only then did he see Callum's men leading Lord Eiloch's forces upon the trail he'd made. He breathed easier when they took the bait, for it meant they had not found Celeste.

Impatience pulled at him to go to her, to bring her out from underground and ensure that she was safe. A vision pulled at his mind, of her arms around him, her body pressed close.

The past few days had worn both of them down, and in the face of the threats surrounding them, there was the need to reaffirm life. To hold her skin against his, daring to reach for a woman he was never supposed to have.

Was it worth it, to kneel before her body to worship, knowing that she might once again walk away? Or could he convince her to look past his poverty to see the man he was?

Celeste didn't know how many hours passed or how long she was waiting in the dim light before the trapdoor swung open.

"Are you all right?" came the voice of Dougal. He climbed down the ladder and helped her back to her feet.

No, she wasn't. But Celeste forced herself to answer yes, despite her chattering teeth. She'd remained beneath the fur coverlet, trying to stay warm. Her hands were numb, her cheeks icy from remaining belowground for so long.

"Come above, and I'll see to it that you get warm." His voice held worry, and he guided her hands to rest upon the ladder rungs.

Her hands stilled upon the wood, and she paused a moment. "What happened to the soldiers?"

His hands encircled her waist, and he gave her a slight nudge, silently encouraging her to climb. "Callum let them search here, while I went riding with Ivory, making a trail to the north. It should keep them occupied for a while."

Though she climbed up a single rung, Celeste turned to face him while his hands remained at her waist. "Will they be back?"

"Not this night," he said. "You can get warm and sleep without fear."

She wasn't certain that was true, but she managed a nod. "Thank you for your help."

"I keep my promises, Celeste. I'll let nothing happen to you."

She stared into his eyes, unable to stop herself from reaching toward his face. Gently, she smoothed a hand over his hair, resting her palm against the back of his head. Standing atop the single rung, it brought her face even to his. He was so close, she could lean in and touch his mouth with hers.

"Don't look at me like that," he warned, his voice in a low growl. Though she was shivering, she saw the flare of desire in his eyes. It was like last night, when he'd warned her of what he would do if he spent the night beside her. Her body softened at the thought of him claiming her, moving with their bodies joined together.

Quickly, she turned away, climbing up the ladder. Her breathing was shallow, her heart quaking within her chest. When she reached the top, Lady Marguerite and Callum were waiting. The light was fading, and Celeste stumbled toward the fire burning in the hearth.

"She's freezing," Dougal told Marguerite. "We need to get her warm."

"I'll arrange for a hot bath," the young woman agreed. To Celeste, she added, "There is a smaller chamber near to mine. I'll have the children sleep down here tonight, and you may have the space to yourself."

Celeste thanked the woman, still rubbing her hands above the fire. Dougal was speaking to his brother, and she watched him from the corner of her eye. They were discussing the men tracking her, and although he'd tried to explain that there was no longer any danger this night, she didn't believe it. They would not abandon the search so easily.

Servants were busy heating water and bringing it above stairs for her bath. The idea of sinking into hot water was near to heaven, and she was eager to get warm. Marguerite offered her a fresh gown to borrow, and Celeste followed the woman up the winding wooden stairs, grateful for it.

"I'll send a maid to tend you in your bath," Marguerite continued. She opened the door to the chamber and welcomed her inside. The servants had already added steaming water to the tub, and another had laid out a linen drying cloth.

"Before I go, I . . . wanted to ask if you and Dougal—" Her words broke away, as if she didn't know how to phrase the question. Embarrassment flushed over the woman's face, and she added, "I don't mean to pry."

Her words voiced a question Celeste didn't know how to answer. In essence, Lady Marguerite was wanting to know if she and Dougal were lovers.

This night, Celeste craved his presence, even if it meant nothing more than sleeping with his arms around her. The comfort and safety Dougal represented were everything.

Keeping her voice in a low whisper, she admitted, "He means a great deal to me."

There. Let her make of that what she wanted. Even if it meant Dougal slept outside her door, it would make her feel better.

Marguerite's expression remained serious. "Dougal has never shown interest in a woman before you." Her gaze fixated upon Celeste. "He is like a brother to me, even if we do not share the same blood."

She did not have to say anything else. There was no doubting the warning in her words. Celeste nodded but met the woman's gaze squarely. "I understand. But I would want him near to me this night."

The servants continued to come and go, filling up the small wooden tub. Steam billowed up into the cool air, and the light was dim, despite the flare of several beeswax candles.

Marguerite helped her to unlace her gown, and within moments Celeste was in the water, up to her chin. She closed her eyes, so grateful for the healing warmth. "I will send someone to you shortly," the lady said before she closed the door behind her.

Dougal held the cake of soap Marguerite had given him. "Knock on the chamber door and give this to the maidservant, if you would." His brother's wife did not wait for him to argue but fled as soon as his hand closed over the soap.

It was a strange bidding, but he supposed she'd forgotten to give it to the maid.

He went up the winding stairs and paused before the doorway. Though he supposed Marguerite would want him to sleep in the Hall with the other men, he fully intended to sleep outside Celeste's door.

If Lord Eiloch's soldiers somehow returned in the night, he wanted to be there to defend her. He and Callum had posted extra guards, with the reminder to the men to alert them at the sign of anyone suspicious.

Dougal knocked upon the door, waiting for the maid to open it. A voice called out for him to enter and his hand stilled upon the latch.

Enter? When they did not know who stood beyond the door? Were they expecting another maid?

Slowly, he lifted the latch, averting his gaze as he waited for the maid to approach. Instead, there was only silence.

He closed the door behind him and when he dared to look, every thought left his brain. Celeste was resting in a tub of water, her hair pinned up, while her bare breasts bobbed atop the water.

"Forgive me," he muttered, turning to go. "I thought a maid was with you to—"

"Wait." Her voice was calm, not at all afraid of him. Dougal froze with his back to her, and in that single word, his imagination filled in the spaces, reminding him of the bare skin he'd glimpsed. She wanted him to wait?

"I wasn't trying to intrude," he said. The steam from her bath made the air heavy, and the aroma of dried herbs filled up the tiny space.

"You weren't intruding." He heard the faint splash of water and though there was hesitation in her voice, she said, "Will you bring me the soap?"

His feet wouldn't move. A rigid desire swelled through him, and he gripped the bar of soap as if it would somehow dispel the dark needs.

"No," he answered after a time. "I'll send someone else."

"And what if I want you?"

The words severed any remaining denial within him, and he dared to turn back. Though her arms now covered her bare breasts, he could see the blush on her cheeks. She was no maiden, for she had known a husband's touch. She knew exactly what she was offering, and God help him, he lacked the willpower to say no. But he would try once more.

"This wasn't part of our arrangement."

She regarded him, her blue eyes capturing his. "Do you want to leave me?"

He'd dreamed of touching that sweet skin, of tasting every inch of her. Of joining their bodies together, sheathing himself inside until she arched with trembling pleasure.

"You don't know what you're asking." He drew nearer, setting the soap down upon the wooden floor. There was a stool beside the tub and he went to sit upon it. From this vantage point, he could see her wet skin glistening against the candlelight.

"Yes, I do. And I don't want to be alone this night. Not when I might die on the morrow."

He understood, then. She wanted a few hours to forget the men pursuing them, to seize a moment of pleasure when it could be her last. He could no more refuse her than he could sever his right arm.

Slowly, Celeste lowered her arms back into the water, revealing her breasts again. Pink-tipped and wet, they were large and tempting. Her nipples were erect, and his body responded with a desire so strong, his groin ached.

He dipped his hands into the hot water and then lathered up his hands. "Sit up," he commanded. She obeyed, and he began by washing her back, sliding his hands over skin so soft, his hands grew slick. Scooping handfuls of water over her back, he rinsed her, and then soaped his hands once more. He caressed her shoulders with the soap, moving his palms down to touch her breasts.

They were a gentle weight, and he drew his thumbs over the pointed nipples, tormenting her as he washed them with the soap. Her hands gripped the edge of the tub, her eyes closed as she allowed him to touch her.

"Please—" she managed to say, gasping as he rinsed away the soap, easing her to sit up. Her nipples had darkened in color, and he gave in to temptation, kissing her deeply as he explored her breasts with both hands. He didn't want her remembering her first husband or anyone else at this moment. Only him.

Though he didn't know what had made her decide to invite him in, his honor had crumbled into dust. There was only Celeste kissing him hard, her tongue touching his while he gripped her above the water. Her hands were pulling at his tunic and he broke free long enough to remove it.

Celeste rose up to her knees in the tub, embracing him skin to skin. He didn't care at all that her body was wet against his own. The sensation of her breasts pressed to him was more arousing than anything he'd ever felt before.

"Slow down," he commanded, pressing her back. "I haven't finished tending you in the bath yet."

She stilled, but her eyes held a passion that mirrored his. "Then do what you will."

She was dying against his touch. Dougal had washed every part of her, paying particular attention to her sensitive breasts. "Before the night is over, I'm going to taste you," he warned.

Heaven help her, she prayed he would. Her body felt alive, as if he was possessing it with every touch, every kiss. Now that his tunic was off, she could see the firm muscles and his hard chest that tapered down to a ridged abdomen.

He used the soap again to wash her feet, his hands moving up one calf. He massaged her skin as he explored her, his hand drifting to her inner thigh. Her breathing was shaky, and the water lapped against her in another caress. Dougal repeated the motions with the other foot, washing her gently until his hand moved between her legs. His fingers rested against her intimate opening, and he palmed her there, his dark eyes locked with hers.

She gasped as his thumb edged her mons, his hand cupping her curls.

"Shall I wash you there?" he demanded.

She couldn't speak, her body was rising so hard. She was utterly pliant against his hand, her breathing hitched as he stroked her. His thumb grazed the hard nodule above her opening, before he slid a finger inside her.

"Is this what you were wanting?" he asked, bending to kiss her mouth. His lips captured her, while below the water he penetrated her with his finger.

Slowly, he added another when she managed to answer a breathless, "Yes."

The steady rhythm was starting to pull at her, and she was afraid of surrendering, unsure of what he was doing. But the more he touched her, the more she leaned in to him, feeling the ache between her legs. His warm mouth enclosed one nipple, and she gripped his head, shaking hard as the sensations intensified.

"Let go," he ordered against her skin, taking the other nipple. "Celeste, stop fighting me."

She didn't know what he wanted, but when he began to suck hard, her fingers dug into his hair. He rubbed against her, his hands demanding a response she couldn't bear.

Then he added another finger, and his thumb pressed her hard. A scorching release soared through her and she cried out, bucking against him as he filled her with his fingers. Her body was like melted tallow, pliant to him.

"I'm sorry. I couldn't stop myself," she murmured, feeling embarrassed at what had happened.

A dark laugh broke through him, and Dougal helped her to stand, wrapping her in the linen drying cloth. "I wanted to pleasure you, Celeste. And we're not finished yet."

She stepped out of the tub, her skin freezing at the cool air. Dougal kept her covered in the linen cloth while he led her toward a small pallet in the corner. It was covered with fur, and he took a moment to dry her off before laying her back against the soft coverlet. He stood before her, his eyes searing as he unfastened his trews and finished undressing.

His body was lean and powerful, his legs muscled from riding. And his manhood was heavy and erect when he knelt down beside her.

"I'm cold," she whispered, beckoning for him to lie atop her. His skin was warmer than she'd expected, and Dougal pulled another coverlet atop both of them. He rested his body weight on his forearms as he stared down at her.

"I don't think this was what you intended when you asked for my protection."

Celeste shook her head but moved her legs apart, bringing his aroused manhood directly in contact with her slick heat.

Although it had never been painful with Edmon, never had she craved his body inside hers.

She wanted to feel Dougal moving within her, and she pressed her hips against his. Yes, this was exactly what she'd hoped for several days ago. But she'd never dreamed it would feel like this. "I trust you," she whispered.

Lifting her knees, she guided him inside her, her body stretching against his fullness. "Yes," she breathed, marveling that it could be this good.

Dougal's face was strained taut, but his mouth trailed down the column of her throat in a wet path to her breasts. As he suckled one, he plunged in deep, intensifying her arousal. She felt the answering pull, her body needing his.

Slowly, he moved within her, a fluid rhythm that felt so good, she pushed back, welcoming the thrust. He raised one of her legs over one hip, and in his eyes, she saw the man she'd loved for so long.

She'd been wrong to leave him. Dougal never would have let anything happen to her, nor would he have let her starve. The two years she'd spent with Edmon paled in comparison to one night with this man.

"More," she urged, holding his hips. He guided her legs around his waist, elevating her hips until he penetrated harder. Over and over he plunged, forcing her to meet each thrust.

"Look at me," he commanded. "I want to see your eyes when I'm inside you."

She did, and the feral look pulled her apart. He was marking her, forcing her to see the man who was pleasuring her. And God above, the intensity was mind-stealing. He was raw and untamed, quickening the pace until she could do nothing but hold fast and surrender.

Liquid heat pulsed inside, and she shuddered, climaxing around him as he continued to drive inside her.

"Let go," she pleaded, grasping his face with her hands. She couldn't bear much more of this. But he only kissed her hard, continuing the relentless rhythm. As if he was trying to drive out the memories of any man but him.

She couldn't catch her breath, for it was coming in swift gasps, until at last he came in a fierce thrust. His breath shuddered as he pumped inside her, his arms gripping her hard.

Their bodies were joined in a way that made a mockery of what her marriage had been. *This* was what it meant to share a man's bed. She'd never known, and though Dougal was still buried deep within her, there was a joy that he'd awakened.

"I liked that," she murmured with a lazy smile, pulling him into a kiss. But neither of them spoke of what the morrow would bring. And she could not say what would happen anymore.

There could be a child, a memory of this night. A child who would save both her and her sister. A wild hope filled her, that perhaps she could have everything. She could reclaim Eiloch and later bring Dougal back to stay with her.

But when he rolled over, curling his body around hers, a sense of darkness surrounded her. No. He would never give his child another man's name. If he knew that she had wanted him in her bed for that purpose, he would never forgive her.

Once again, she would have to choose, for she could not have both.

Dougal awoke in the middle of the night to find Celeste naked in his arms. Her body was warm, her hair tangled down her back. He stroked the length of it, and her mouth pressed a sleepy kiss against his chest.

Though he'd grown hard and his shaft was demanding more, he held back. She was not a virgin, and he could claim her again if she would have him. And yet . . . even though he'd sated his lust, he'd sensed that there was more at play here. She'd had a reason for inviting him into her bed, and he could not guess what it was.

He moved her atop him, enjoying the sensation of her naked body against his. He caressed her skin, down her spine to her round bottom. Almost immediately, his shaft surged against her.

"Is it morning?" she murmured, raising her head.

"Not yet." He reached up to explore her skin, and she startled him when she raised up, easing his erection against her. She wasn't entirely ready for him, but he stroked her, kindling the response he wanted. She was tentative, almost hesitant in the way she held herself. But as her body relaxed, he felt the wetness between her legs. This time, when she pressed herself upon him, she welcomed him inside.

"We can't stay here," she whispered. "Your brother said we have to leave before dawn."

"Soon." He lifted her up, reveling when she sank down against him. As she moved in rhythm, he was torn between wanting to hear her cry out in release . . . and questioning why she had chosen to lie with him.

Aye, it was an intense pleasure, one he welcomed. But he suspected that this time together would come to an end.

Dougal disengaged from her, never minding that he was brutally aroused, his body slick with her wetness. She misunderstood what he wanted and instead rolled to her side, her hand curling around his shaft. Carefully, she guided him back inside her, but the new position didn't bring him deep enough. He guided her onto her hands and knees, reaching to cup her breasts while he entered her from behind.

For a moment he teased the hard nipples, feeling the way she clenched at him within her depths. But when she backed against him, he forgot what he was doing and lost himself as he grasped her hips firmly and claimed her.

Mine, he thought savagely as he invaded and withdrew. He wanted to brand himself within her, to shatter apart her senses until she remembered no man except him. She was meeting him with every thrust, until he grew so hard, he was afraid of harming her.

She lowered her torso to the ground, raising her backside in a way that increased the sweet friction and took him deeper.

Did she think he was simply going to let her go after this?

No. He wanted more than that. He didn't want her to leave him again. Though he would keep his promise to help rescue her sister, the girl's freedom would come at another price.

He wanted Celeste.

He wanted to spend his nights in gloried lovemaking and his days making her happy. He wanted her to admit her mistake, agreeing to come back to Glen Arrin with him. She'd been the woman he'd loved for so long, the woman who knew how to get beneath his skin.

And when she was crying out in wicked release, begging him to end the torment, he filled her with his seed, collapsing atop her.

Nothing would force him to let her go. Not after this.

Chapter Six

In the darkness, Celeste put on the gown Marguerite had loaned her. Dougal was sleeping hard, his naked body revealed against the fur pallet. It was quiet within the fortress, and she wanted a few moments alone.

They had spent too long together, making love. She'd been unable to resist him, and now there was no time to escape, no time to ride away with him. She stepped into her shoes, closing the door behind her.

Within the fortress, every archer stood on the battlements, their bows at the ready. Callum was among them, and as soon as Marguerite spied her, she pulled her back inside.

"Don't. They'll see you."

But Celeste ignored the woman, moving along the wall until she reached a crevice that allowed her to see outside the fortress. Lord Eiloch's soldiers were waiting, surrounding them on all sides. There was no means of escaping them without bloodshed. And it was her fault for drawing them here.

She leaned back against the wall, understanding that many lives would be lost. Possibly even Dougal's, if they dared to fight back.

From behind, she heard footsteps. Dougal had awakened and dressed so quickly his tunic hung open.

"Stay with Marguerite," he ordered. "We have archers. And Callum is better than all of them. They won't make it past the gates."

"After you've killed them, Rowena will send an army here. They'll butcher your family." She had no doubt of it, and dismay flooded through her at the thought. She'd brought them away from Glen Arrin, only to increase the threat to Cairnross. They wouldn't give up.

But Dougal's gaze hardened. "They won't if we kill them first."

She could not allow him to start a war. Turning to face him, she saw the fervor in his eyes. He intended to fight for her, no matter what the cost.

"No." She moved past him, toward Marguerite. To the woman, she asked, "I want to invite Lord Eiloch inside. I would speak with him now and see if we can come to an agreement without any fighting." It was time to stop running and do what she could to save them.

"Only if he comes alone," Dougal said. "His men must stay beyond the gates."

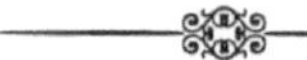

Lord Eiloch rested his hand upon his sword when he entered. Dougal remained at Celeste's side, uncertain why she was surrendering so easily. Did she not believe he could defend her? His anger was barely in check, and he was itching for a fight. If the man made one move to harm her, he'd find himself dead.

"I know why you left," Lord Eiloch began, his gaze fixed upon Celeste. "But it won't work."

He raised his eyes to Dougal and a smug look crossed his face. To Celeste, he added, "I suppose you took him as your lover, didn't you? You thought to conceive a child and pass your bastard off as Edmon's."

The stricken look on Celeste's face was worse than a blow to Dougal's stomach. It spoke of a truth he'd never imagined. A child? Was that the reason she'd come this far?

When he sent her a questioning look, tears formed in her eyes. And when he glanced at her, they were tears of guilt.

A numbness settled through him, for he'd never imagined she would use him in that way. Was she already pregnant when he'd lain with her last night? Or was Lord Eiloch speaking the truth, that she'd lain with him to conceive a son?

"I sought sanctuary with the MacKinlochs," Celeste said quietly. "Because your wife tried to murder any child I might have conceived."

A darkness clouded his judgment, and Dougal hardly heard the rest of the conversation. All he could think of was the way she'd behaved these past few days. She *had* kissed him first and had tempted him each moment they were alone. Even last night, she'd asked him to tend her in the bath, knowing it would lead to a night of lovemaking.

A night where she intended to steal a child from him.

She used you. She never wanted you at all, any more than any woman ever has. Even your own mother didn't want you.

The words taunted him, digging into his conscience. As an adolescent, he'd poured his rage and grief into fighting, lashing out at anyone and everyone. But it had done nothing to heal the emptiness there. After his brothers were freed, it had calmed his unrest, but still he preferred solitude.

He'd been a fool to think that Celeste might love him. And he deserved the humiliating shame she'd evoked.

His anger was so strong, he began to walk away. If he stayed another moment, he couldn't trust himself not to lash out with with words he'd regret later. But right now he didn't care what Celeste did or where she went.

The door struck hard behind him, but he continued his path forward. She could go or stay; it made no difference anymore.

Dougal made it as far as the stable, where he took Ivory out of the stall, preparing her to ride. But hurried footsteps approached, and he was well aware that Celeste wasn't about to let him leave without confronting him.

"Lionel was wrong about what he said." She stood in front of the doorway to block him from leaving.

He stepped back from the horse, moving closer. "I don't believe you. At every moment we were alone, you offered yourself. I should have known better."

She paled and lowered her gaze. "I let go of that idea within a day. It was a desperate thought, one I couldn't bring myself to do."

The lies were an acid, burning at his mood. She stood there like a martyr, willing to sacrifice herself to save his family. He closed in, bringing her back against the wooden stall. "And last night, you decided to lower yourself after all. To me, a man you would never consider marrying."

"You're wrong," she said, her hands clenched at her sides. "I loved you. I still do."

"You've gotten good at lying." He led Ivory forward, stopping in front of her. "Is that why you invited me in your bed? To steal a child and pass him off as your dead husband's?"

She shook her head slowly. But he couldn't believe a treacherous word she said. He pushed his way past her, taking Ivory outside.

"Dougal, don't go," she pleaded.

"Why not? Because you want me to continue warming your bed until you find a man worth marrying?"

She gripped her waist as if he'd struck her. A tear spilled over, but she didn't stop him when he took the horse. Nor did she say a single word when he left her standing there.

He never wanted to lay eyes upon her again.

Three days later

She should have known Dougal would despise her after what she'd done. And though the night she'd spent in his arms had been her choice, he wouldn't believe it after Lord Eiloch's words. Worst of all was the bleak emptiness stretching before her. She'd never expected to feel so alone, as if she was walking away from hope.

Celeste saw no choice but to return with Lord Eiloch. He would only fight against Dougal's family if she dared refuse.

No longer did she care about her widow's portion of Edmon's estates. She was weary of the scheming and living her life in fear.

"I will return with you of my own will," she told Lionel. "Leave the MacKinlochs in peace, and I'll surrender my husband's lands to you. All I ask is that you allow me to take my sister away with horses and a few of our belongings."

"What of any child you might bear?" he asked, his voice threaded with wariness. "That was your intent when you left, was it not?"

She met his gaze evenly. "If I were to have a child, it would not be your brother's," she admitted. "There is nothing to stop you from claiming Eiloch as yours. I will swear to that."

His posture relaxed visibly, and she was startled when she sensed an apology in his tone. "It was never my intent to force you out of your home."

"I am not wanted there," she said. "Rowena would make our lives a misery."

He looked away for a moment, as if he'd known it. "She is a difficult woman to understand. She holds great ambitions, and she would lay down her life for one of our children."

She would lay down my life, too, thought Celeste, but she didn't say it.

"Where will you go when you bring Melisandre with you?" Lionel asked, keeping his horse beside hers. "Back to Glen Arrin?"

"Perhaps." She believed Nairna and Laren might grant her sanctuary. And although she had wounded Dougal's pride, she wanted a second chance.

The thought of walking away, of never seeing him again, upset her in a way she'd never expected. He'd left her behind and likely would never forgive her for what she'd done. She ought to simply let him go.

But she didn't want to. Not like this, with him loathing the sight of her. She'd made mistakes and needed to atone for them. And more than that, if there was a child after their night together, he deserved to know about it. Pretending it hadn't happened was a coward's path.

He wouldn't want to see her. It was entirely possible that he'd refuse to speak with her again. Unless...

A sudden thought struck her with a jolt of hope. It was entirely too soon to tell whether a child had resulted from their stolen night together. And perhaps she could stay with Dougal, for a time, until they knew for certain. At least, long enough to gain his forgiveness and to show him that she truly did love him.

Her imagination fired up with determination. This time, she would fight for the man she wanted.

It was a fortnight before she returned to Glen Arrin with her sister. Celeste rode her husband's Arabian stallion, Titan, while

Melisandre took a tamer gelding. Titan was black with a white star on his forehead and white markings above his hooves. He was slightly larger than Dougal's mare and was more difficult to manage. All through the journey, the animal was stubborn, trying to take her in whatever direction he wanted.

"Dougal is welcome to you," she informed the stallion. In answer to her remark, the horse veered left and began to graze.

Melisandre smirked. "He has a mind of his own, doesn't he?"

Celeste dismounted and seized Titan's reins, guiding him away from the grass and forcing him back onto the path. "Not for long. Once Dougal gets him, he'll make him behave."

Though she spoke as if it were nothing, inwardly she was nervous. The last time she'd seen Dougal, he'd been furious with her. He might not believe anything she said.

"And he...wants you back, even after all that's happened?" Her sister was well aware of her feelings toward Dougal. There were days when Melisandre seemed much wiser than a girl of three and ten.

"We made our peace," was all she could say. But with each mile they drew closer, her pulse quickened with fear.

Melisandre looked doubtful. "What if the MacKinlochs refuse to let us stay? Where will we go?"

"They won't turn us away," she assured her. "But even if they did, we could always appeal to the Baron of Locharr."

Celeste refused to consider failure. Dougal would be angry, but she would not let him go a second time. The true question was whether he would set aside his pride and forgive her.

They continued riding until they reached the gates. Once they arrived, Lord Eiloch's men departed, leaving them to stand there alone.

To the guards, Celeste said, "I've brought a gift for Dougal MacKinloch." They recognized her from the earlier visit and allowed her to enter. But once she and Melisandre were past the gates, she sensed a chill in the atmosphere. There were stares in her direction but no smiles.

"They don't seem happy to see us," Melisandre whispered.

Celeste dismounted and led the stallion forward. There were people tending sheep and others milling about. Though she greeted a few of them, none answered her.

At the bottom of the stairs leading into the castle stood Nairna. The woman's face was grave, her green eyes wary. Celeste suspected Dougal had told his family the very worst about her.

"I came to uphold my part of the agreement," she said to Nairna, holding out the horse. "I promised Dougal this stallion."

"He does not wish to see you," the woman answered.

She knew. Somehow Nairna had guessed what had happened between them. But Celeste hadn't journeyed this far to give up.

"Is he here?" she asked gently. "There is something he needs to know. I must speak with him."

"He is, but I will honor his wishes. You've brought the horse, and you can go back to Eiloch." Nairna's words were like frost, and her warning was clear: *Hurt a MacKinloch man, and there is no place for you here.*

But they could not return to Eiloch. She had given up everything to come here, and there was no turning back. Celeste closed her hand over Melisandre's and regarded Nairna. "I don't know what he told you, but if I could just see him . . . "

"He knows you are here. If he wants to see you, he will." Nairna took the reins of the horse. "I'll bring the stallion to him."

She made no offer of hospitality or a place to rest. Celeste stood frozen while the woman took the horse away.

Melisandre dismounted from her own animal, wariness written all over her face. "I thought we would be living here."

"I suppose I was wrong." Celeste could find no words to ease her sister's fear, for her own worries were drowning her. They had a little food, but not much. It would be dark within hours, and they needed a place to sleep. It was half a day's journey to Locharr, too far to reach the fortress by tonight.

"I don't know what you said or did," her younger sister remarked, "but let me try." Melisandre walked forward with her own horse, adding, "I'll bring my horse to the stable and find out what I can. If you think it's safe?"

Celeste nodded. "No one will harm you. And in the meantime, I'll see if I can find Dougal." They split off, and she walked back toward his home. She could only pray that he was there and would agree to talk to her.

She made it halfway before she saw Dougal walking forward. His hair was slightly longer, his face unshaven and rough. He wore trews and a saffron shirt, and two dirks were strapped to him—one within a leather belt and another at his shoulder. His dark brown eyes stared past her, as if she wasn't even there. Celeste held her ground, refusing to back down.

"I brought you the stallion."

Dougal said nothing but continued walking forward. His fury was palpable, and she hurried forward to catch up to him.

"Well, at the very least you should thank me. He's an expensive horse."

Her words had the intended effect. He spun, his eyes blazing. "Thank you? For demanding that I be your escort and trying to steal a child from me, to pass off as your husband's?"

He moved in so fast, she lost her breath when he seized her shoulders. "I let no one use me, *Lady* Celeste. And if you think I want anything at all from you, you're wrong."

"I left Eiloch and gave up everything to my husband's brother," she said quietly. "To come to you."

"There is no place for you here," he countered. "Not after what you did."

Her own temper erupted at that. "And what did I do that was so wrong? I went to seek help for my sister in any way that I could. Don't tell me you wouldn't lay down your life for one of your brothers."

"It's not the same."

"No, because you aren't a woman. I came to you for help, and I offered you the payment you wanted. I kept my word."

"You used me."

She drew herself up to her full height, glaring at him. "I didn't hear you saying no to me that night. You enjoyed every moment of it, and that's what angers you most. Because you still want me, even after all that."

She rested her hand upon his throat and could feel his rapid pulse beneath her fingers. "It was my choice to lie with you that night. And I never stole anything from you. I returned and kept my promise, just as I said I would."

"I don't want you, Celeste. I'll accept the horse, but that's all I want from you. You're nothing to me."

He walked away, leaving her to stand there alone. Tears welled up inside her, and she turned away to let them fall. Better to release them now, where no one would see, than to be weak before her sister. Melisandre needed her to be strong. They had to gain shelter and somehow survive this.

But she simply didn't know how to break down the stony pride of a man who hated her.

"Do you want me to send her away?" Laren asked while Dougal examined the stallion Celeste had brought. "She traveled a long way to see you." His brother's wife kept her voice even, but he sensed her frustration. She was dying to ask him what had happened, but he would say nothing.

Just remembering that night made him feel like a fool. Celeste had invited him into her bath, using her body and words to seduce him. He'd been such a fool, only too eager to touch her, to sheathe himself in her body and watch her crumble.

Had she ever wanted him? Or had she merely schemed to conceive a child to protect herself from her husband's brother? He didn't know.

After he'd left her, she'd gone back to Eiloch without a second thought. She'd returned with her enemy, leaving him to wonder if she was even alive.

And now that he'd seen her again, he craved her even more. Seeing her here, with her golden-brown hair pinned beneath a veil, her blue gown accentuating a slender waist, made him want to drag her back home again.

He loathed himself for the weakness.

"Dougal?" Laren questioned again. "She brought her sister and wants to stay." The woman moved forward to stand at his side. "But Nairna thinks she should go back."

She was leaving the decision up to him, but he knew what her wishes would be. "You don't want to send them away."

Laren shook her head. "I spoke with Melisandre for a short while. She said that Celeste gave up all rights to her land, to return to you."

He said nothing, refusing to believe any of it.

His brother's wife touched his arm, asking gently, "Why do you fight your feelings for her? I can see in your face how much it hurt when she left."

"I knew she would leave me." Every woman he'd ever known had left; why would Celeste be any different?

"She came back," Laren said. "And I think you should give her another chance. At least hear what she has to say."

"She gave me nothing but lies, Laren. Why would I want to hear more?"

The young woman let out a sigh. "Stubbornness runs in MacKinloch blood." She stood on tiptoe and kissed his cheek. "Her sister can sleep with my girls this night."

"And what of Lady Eiloch?" he demanded, unable to stop himself from asking.

"Where do *you* want me to send her?" Without waiting for a reply, Laren walked away.

Dougal grimaced, for he knew he would find Celeste in his dwelling. The question was whether or not he'd have the willpower to turn her away. Or whether he should.

CHAPTER SEVEN

Celeste stood within the fence boundaries while the stallion explored his new home. Dougal kept his mare, Ivory, separated, but the animal appeared nervous at the arrival of the new horse. In one hand, he held a carrot, intending to entice Titan with it. The stallion was fully aware of him but showed more interest in grazing.

"You shouldn't be here," Dougal warned Celeste. "He's nervous already."

"I traveled with him all the way here," she countered. Her blue eyes fixed upon him, and she added, "He's the most stubborn creature I've ever met. He won't listen to anything I say."

He thought he detected an undertone beneath her words. "Horses can sense when a rider is not in command."

"It doesn't matter what I say or do. He's made up his mind already." She went to stand beside him, and crossed her arms. "He doesn't understand that I only wanted to take care of him."

"Are we still talking about horses?" He risked a glance, and the glare in her eyes was unmistakable.

"I gave up my land to keep a promise to you. And it seems I made the wrong choice, since you're determined that I should not stay here."

"Laren is Lady of Glen Arrin. She'll give you a place for the night until you can go."

"Is that what you want? For us to leave and never return?"

"Yes." He spoke without thinking, but the words held a note of falsehood. When he was around Celeste, he hardly knew himself anymore. He wanted her in his arms, her mouth upon his. He wanted to awaken beside her in the morning and fall asleep with her at night.

She was his greatest weakness, and he didn't want to trust her again. When he'd allowed himself to believe, for a moment, that she'd wanted him, he'd felt a sense of wholeness. As if there was someone who would stand by him, who needed him. When Lord Eiloch had offered the ugly truth, it had only confirmed what he'd feared—that she'd only wanted to use him.

"Just a few days," she murmured, lifting her face to his in a wordless plea. "If you cannot forgive me, then I'll go."

He didn't want to try again. For he sensed that if he took even a single step forward, he would end up in her bed once more. Celeste de Laurent was like a sorceress, binding him to her until there was nothing left of himself.

She took his hand in hers. "We could go for a ride if you want. I could take Ivory, and you could ride Titan."

"Ivory is still getting used to having a saddle," he argued. "She's not safe for you."

"Then I'll see what I can do to tame that beast of a horse. I'll ride Titan, if I must." She sent him a slight smile. "We could race them."

"I'd win." He pointed toward the stallion, who was still grazing. "Your mount is more interested in food."

"That could change, if he's running alongside the female. He might try to chase her." She straightened and offered, "I'll make you a wager on it."

"And what do you want if you win?" Although he doubted if her stallion would obey her enough to win the race, he wondered what she would ask for.

"I want to stay at Glen Arrin," she said, "with my sister."

Already she was taking the stallion by the bridle, leading him away from the grass. She spoke to him in a firm tone, as if trying to convince the animal to win. Dougal went to retrieve Ivory, amused by the way she was chiding the stallion.

"What do you want from me if you win?" she asked.

He helped her saddle Titan again, then boosted her up. "You already know what I want."

Her face dimmed. "Don't ask me to leave, Dougal." The hurt look in her eyes made him feel like a bastard. But damn her, why should he let her stay? He had no desire to be tormented by her presence each day, reminded of the way she'd seduced him and cast him aside.

Celeste dug her heels into the stallion and urged him out toward the open fields. Without even waiting for him, she started the race. Cheating, was she?

He had to hurry to saddle Ivory and then catch up to her. Celeste had gained a strong lead, and as she took the stallion north, Dougal marveled at how well Titan ran.

Ivory raced to catch up, and the mare began to close the distance. Although Titan was a fast stallion, Celeste wasn't as skilled a rider. She was also racing toward the edge of another loch. Dougal followed her, and soon enough, their horses were side by side.

He could pull ahead and win the race. But something held him back. Ivory, however, had other ideas, and began to force her way to the front. Celeste appeared dismayed and leaned forward, urging the horse even faster.

But the stallion had grown winded and was already slowing down.

"Come on!" she urged, but Ivory had pulled all the way ahead of them while Titan had slowed to a trot. When she tried again to move him forward, the horse reared up, sending her flying into the water.

He'd won.

Dougal wheeled the horse around and hurried back to where she'd been thrown. Celeste trudged through the waist-high water, glaring at the stallion. The animal nickered at her, and she was so angry, she flicked water at it. "You are welcome to him, for he's a horrible creature."

Her hair was sodden from the water, her gown plastered to her body. Dougal couldn't stop the laugh that rumbled from inside him. He dismounted, holding on to Ivory's reins.

"Don't you dare laugh," she warned. "I don't know why I ever thought this was a good idea."

"I warned you." His grin was so broad, she dipped her hands in the water and slung a wave at him. The water doused him in the face, dripping down his shirt, but he hardly cared as he laughed even harder. "Next time you need someone to tend you in the bath, I'll send my horse."

"How can you stand there and laugh at me?" she demanded, sloshing through the water until she stood before him. "This isn't at all funny."

Oh, but it was. He reached out for her fallen veil and wrung it out. His shoulders shook as he did, but when he glanced back at Celeste, she was crying. Her face held a lifetime of misery, and she clutched her waist as if she was in pain.

"Were you hurt?" he asked, dropping the veil. She'd struck the water, but had he been wrong? Had she hit her head? He hurried to her, not knowing whether he should touch her or not.

"It w-wasn't supposed to happen like this," she sobbed. "I thought when I returned that you'd be glad to see me. That you'd want your horse."

"I did want my horse."

"But you wanted to be rid of *me*," she wept.

He was so dumbfounded by her reaction, he raked a hand through his hair, wondering what to say. Before he could think of anything, she started pouring out her woes.

"I don't know why I ever thought I should return to you. It was awful at Eiloch, but at least I had a place to sleep at night."

"Until they tried to kill you," he felt compelled to point out.

Celeste stepped closer to him, so near he let her come into his embrace where she pressed her face against his heart. "You made me feel safe. And I don't care what Lionel said to you—it wasn't true. I never would have taken a child from you. At least . . . not without coming back."

Every word he'd been meaning to say froze within his throat. Was that the reason she'd returned? "You're not having a child, are you?" He drew back to look at her.

"I don't know. Perhaps not. Or maybe I am. But even if I was, you'd never want to see me again." She wiped at her eyes and tried to step back.

Before she could move away, he slid his arms around her waist and drew her in again. "You'll stay here until we know if there is a child."

She let out a slow breath. Her eyes were wet and red-rimmed. "Will you forgive me for what I did, Dougal?"

He went motionless, realizing that she was not speaking only of the time during the past fortnight. She was talking of the choice she'd made, to wed Edmon de Laurent.

Her face flushed, but she reached up to touch his cheek. "You have a terrible temper, and you're as stubborn as that wretched stallion. But you're the only man I want. And . . ." She mumbled something against his chest that he couldn't quite hear.

"And what?" He tipped her chin up, certain he'd misheard her. "Say it again."

"I never stopped loving you," she whispered. "With every moment I spent at your side, I wanted another day. I can't imagine being with anyone else."

He searched her face to know if there was truth in her words. When she tried to pull away again, he held her fast. "You're going to drive me to madness if I let you stay, aren't you?"

A hopeful smile touched her mouth. "I want to stay, Dougal. But only with you."

His mouth came down upon hers, as if he'd needed the words. Celeste wound her arms around his neck, their tongues tangled together as he warmed her wet skin with his body. "You need dry clothes," he said. "We're going back."

"Or you could build a fire here," she said. To convince him, she kissed him again, pulling his body as close as she dared. The need to be with him again, to feel his body against hers, was taking apart her inhibitions. His hands were moving over her, and despite the chill of her wet clothes, she was feeling warmer with his touch.

"No. We're returning to Glen Arrin," he said.

"Why?"

"Because if I don't, I'm going to lay you on the ground right here." He lifted her onto Titan's saddle, and then startled her by swinging up behind. He took Ivory's reins and tied them to the saddle, walking the mare behind them.

"Why did you do that?" she asked.

He sent her a wicked smile. "So I can touch you during our ride." Against her bottom, she felt the rise of his erection.

"There's no need to rush," she said, reaching back to touch him. "It might take a while before we reach the fortress." Her palm curled around his length, and he sucked in a breath of air when she rubbed him.

"Are you wanting to play, *a chrìdhe?*" he asked, sliding one hand beneath her wet skirts. The warmth of his palm against her bare skin was shocking, and she inhaled sharply when another hand stroked her breast. She felt him unfasten the ties of his trews, and a moment later, his hot shaft was pressed against the base of her bottom.

The touch of him made her achingly wet. "I don't know if I can wait until we get back," she murmured, groaning when his fingers teased her nipple. She was grateful that the stallion was walking slowly, allowing Dougal to touch her intimately. He cupped her, and she was so wet, she reached back and lifted herself up to guide him inside her body.

For a moment, he remained sheathed within her while the horse walked. The slight motion of the animal made her shift against him, and she shuddered at the tight sensation. If anyone saw them, they would see only her skirts covering his legs. No one would know that they were joined together in lovemaking, and Dougal thrust against her, using the horse's gait to ease the penetration.

Inside, her body was throbbing against him. She'd never felt anything so exquisite as his body within her, until he nudged the horse lightly and sent Titan into a trot. Now the rhythm was bolder, and Dougal forced her to rise up while he thrust and withdrew.

"You're riding both of us," he said against her ear, using one hand to stroke her breast while he plunged against her. "Don't fall off."

It was a fight to keep her balance while he slid so easily within her, and with every bounce of the horse, the nerves within her gathered tightly, rising hard. She sat upon him, letting him fill her deeply, thrusting over and over.

"Dougal," she moaned, and he doubled his rhythm, grasping her waist and slamming her against him. Her hands dug into the horse's mane as he filled her, forcing her to grind against him until she went liquid and convulsed around him.

"More," he ordered, changing the horse's rhythm back to a walk again, until she was breathless, accepting his hard invasion over and over. She was crying out, but he never stopped his thrusts, pushing into her until at last he let out a shuddering breath and took his own release. Even when the horse continued to move, the aftershocks made her clench around his shaft.

He kissed her neck, and remained inside her while they continued the journey back. "I'm not wanting to start over, Celeste. I want to continue on, where we left off."

"Then you've forgiven me?" She drew his arms around her, feeling as if a weight had lifted from her shoulders.

"I said many things out of anger the morning you left. But you were gone before I could come to my senses." He nuzzled her neck before he withdrew from her body at last and fumbled with his trews to fasten them again. Even when he adjusted her skirts, she could feel his body pressed close. "I'll admit, I have a few faults. Not too many, though."

She laughed at that, drawing his arms close. "You're a hot-headed man," she said. Tilting her head back, she added, "Hot-blooded, too, I'd say."

"With you, I am." His mouth moved up to her ear, and she trembled at the warm breath against her skin.

"I want to ride faster with you," she said. "Take me home, Dougal."

He urged the stallion on, holding her close. Ivory kept up with their pace, and there was beauty in the sight of the two horses running together. Celeste felt so alive in his arms, she could hardly piece together any thoughts.

When they reached the outskirts of Glen Arrin, he lifted her down. Then, he took her hand in his and led her back to his home. The interior was dim, and he took a few moments to light the peat fire. She saw the simple pallet on one side, while there was a wooden table and bench on the other. In the small space, she held him tightly.

"I don't have much to offer you, Celeste," he admitted. "This is all I have."

There had been a time when she'd been afraid to return to a simple life. But now, she realized how very much she loved this man. "I don't care where we live, Dougal. So long as you're with me." She kissed him hard, holding him fast. "I know I'll always be safe with you."

"Stay with me," he said, drawing his arms around her.

Celeste rested her hands upon his heart. "You told me I have to stay until we know if there's a bairn growing inside me. What if there isn't?"

"Then we'll have to keep trying until there is." He lifted her into his arms and held her close. "No matter how long it takes."

Epilogue

The foal stood on wobbly legs while Ivory licked her newborn. Celeste smiled at the young animal, while Dougal seemed relieved that the birth had gone well. The baby horse had a blend of white-and-black markings, and his mother nuzzled close.

"He's going to be strong and fast, like his father," she predicted. Seeing the newborn foal made her heart ache, for within the next month, she hoped to hold their own baby.

Dougal stood back and wrapped his arms around her, his hands upon her swollen middle. He stroked their unborn child, dropping a kiss against her jaw. "I believe so, aye."

She lifted her face to his, and turned to embrace him, smiling. "I have to stand sideways to hold you now. And I haven't seen my feet in weeks."

He kissed her, his palm upon her hardened womb. "So long as you're in my arms, it doesn't matter, *a ghràidh*."

She touched his cheek, so thankful for the gift of this man. They had wed at the end of last summer, and it had not taken long before she'd discovered her pregnancy. Although their life together had been simple, she had found joy with Dougal. He never failed to provide for her, and when she wasn't helping him with the horses, she'd joined Nairna and Laren, helping them with various tasks at Glen Arrin.

"Melisandre made a discovery yesterday," she told Dougal. "Do you remember the chest belonging to my father?"

"Lord Eiloch sent it back to you a few days ago."

"Yes. Melisandre and I had left it behind when we came here. It was empty, but Lionel thought we might want it. At least—" she paused and withdrew a leather pouch "—we thought it was empty."

Dougal took the pouch and poured the contents into his hand. Seven gemstones—rubies, emeralds and pearls lay in his hand. "Where did you get these?"

"Melisandre found a hidden panel in the chest. The gemstones were inside it." She'd been so startled by the discovery, she didn't know what to do with their newfound riches. "I never thought my father had any wealth at all."

Dougal replaced the stones and handed them back to her. "These did not come from your father, Celeste."

She stared at him, "Then how did they get there?"

"It was Lord Eiloch's way of replacing your lost inheritance. Without his wife's knowledge."

She sobered and tucked the gems away. It seemed strange to think of Lionel as their benefactor. "Do you think so?"

He nodded, taking her hand and leading her back home. "And it might be that Lady Marguerite's father, the Duc D'Avignois, pointed out to Lord Eiloch that he was behaving like a common thief."

Realization dawned over her that Dougal was responsible. The knowing smile on his face gave it away. "You did this," she said. "Admit it."

"I promised you on our wedding morn that I would take care of you. For always." He opened the door to their home where their peat fire had died down to coals. "You'll never starve or want for anything."

She reached up to him, touching his face. "I know that."

His hands came to cover hers, and he leaned in to her. "I love you, Celeste."

"And I love you." She rested her cheek against his heart, feeling the blessing of this second chance. "We'll save the jewels for Melisandre's dowry. Or perhaps our daughter's, if it's a girl."

He took them from her and set them aside. "I would lay the world at your feet," he said. With a mischievous smile, he added, "That is, if I could *find* your feet." He knelt down and touched her swollen ankles. "Oh, wait. There they are."

"I cannot believe you said that." She rolled her eyes at him, but in his face she saw a gleam of laughter that echoed in her heart. "It's good that I love you, Dougal."

And when he led her back to their bed, she knew that her husband was the best choice she'd ever made.

Keep reading to enjoy an excerpt of Michelle's newest release, *Her Warrior's Redemption.*

Excerpt of Her Warrior's Redemption

Byzantium, 1208

Brian of Penrith walked alongside the men of his traveling party while the sun blazed against his face. The ground seemed to sway beneath his feet after traveling by ship for the past few weeks. His shoes were cracked and worn, his skin burned from the relentless heat. He'd traveled for nearly a year, all the way to Byzantium. Or what had once been Byzantium after the sacking of Constantinople, he supposed. He'd heard rumors about the land being divided up since the Crusade had ended, but it meant nothing to him anymore. He hadn't joined this caravan to fight for God.

No, this was his penance, to atone for his sins. His best friend Robert was dead—all because Brian had lost control of his temper, acting recklessly without thinking. He couldn't bear to stay and witness the grief on his sister's face, for she had loved Robert more than life itself.

It was your fault. You deserve this suffering.

And so, he'd willingly accepted the endless days of exhaustion and hunger. He didn't really know what he was searching for beyond absolution.

He'd traded one group of travelers for another until he'd found another caravan returning to Constantinople. Some were mercenaries while others were merchants seeking their fortune. But he'd joined them on their journey, hoping to find a new purpose. Or, at the very least, an escape.

The hills of the city were like nothing he'd ever seen before. Massive domes and towers guarded the city being rebuilt after the Crusade. The scent of wood and ashes permeated the air, but some of the surviving buildings were gilded, revealing the owner's wealth. Despite the ruins, it surprised him to see baskets and containers of bright flowers. Nearby, a group of men unloaded clay containers of wine from another ship at port.

One of the merchants came to walk alongside him, and he passed Brian a skin of water. "We'll arrive in Constantinople by nightfall. I know a man who can give you a place to stay."

"I've no coins," Brian started to say, but the merchant raised a hand.

"You'll work for him and earn your place." With a sly smile, he added. "You want to learn to fight, don't you? This man knows how to train the strongest fighters in the kingdom." He reached out and pinched Brian's arm. "He can turn you from the weak insect you are into one of the greatest warriors in the world."

Brian jerked away from the man, embarrassed by his lack of strength. He already knew how to fight, though he'd grown too thin on the journey. Robert and his half-brother Piers had trained him as a boy, teaching him some of their techniques, though he'd never had the chance to master them. But he remembered.

No one knew of his fighting abilities, for the long journey and the meager food had taken their toll. The merchant was right. He *was* weak, for he hadn't fought in over a year.

Yet the man's words resonated within him. What if *this* could become his new purpose—to become a fighter and defend those weaker than himself? The idea was appealing, for he'd always admired warriors who could protect others.

"Well?" the merchant prompted. "Do you want to learn to fight?"

Brian met his gaze. "Yes."

"Good." The merchant nodded his approval. "You'll come with me tonight and join the others. We'll get a meal in your belly before you begin."

He would stay for a time, Brian decided. Long enough to get stronger and fill out the muscles he lacked. And perhaps the fighting would grant him the skills he needed to become someone else—a man of honor.

Hours later, Brian met the owner of the arena where the fighters trained. The man, Kadir al-Kumar, was large and ungainly with a long black beard and dark eyes. He spoke no English, but the merchant conversed with him easily in the Byzantine tongue. Brian didn't understand what they said, but Kadir passed a stack of coins to the merchant.

They were continuing to argue when he suddenly felt a hand on his shoulder. A female voice whispered at his ear. "You need to leave. Now."

He turned and saw a servant girl holding a pitcher. She appeared to be the same age as himself, and her light brown hair was bound back in a braid, revealing sun-kissed streaks of gold. Blue eyes stared into his with a warning, and her mouth tightened in unspoken fear.

It startled him to see someone from his homeland here, especially a maiden who spoke his language. He kept his voice low and averted his gaze so as not to draw attention. "How did you come to be here?"

"I've no time to tell that tale. Just . . . heed my warning and leave, as soon as you can." Her voice was tinged with desperation, and he wondered why.

"They told me I could come here to train," he insisted. "I want to learn."

"Not here, you don't." She pretended to fill his cup, keeping her voice low. "They're not who you think they are. Kadir is buying you. You're to become his slave."

Brian narrowed his gaze on the men. They were laughing, and the merchant pulled out a set of dice for gambling. Though he didn't want to believe such a thing was possible, he couldn't ignore her warning. "Why would he want to buy me?"

"For his fighting pits," she said dully. "You're English, like me. Many citizens would pay good coins to watch us fight and die."

He stole another look at the men, wondering if she was right. The merchant had warned him that the Byzantine people still hated the crusaders who had sacked the city.

"I have nowhere else to go," he admitted. "And no silver."

"You have your freedom," she said. "That's worth more than any coins."

Though he didn't want to believe her, she had no reason to lie to him. She reached for his cup and pretended again to fill it. "Find the house with three crosses above the door. A Norman lord lives there, Alexander Berys, Baron Staunton. If you see him, ask him to help free me."

"Where can I find the house?" he asked.

"Look for the Hagia Sophia church. It's the largest in the city. He lives not far from there, west of the church, so he says."

He guessed she'd never been there. Likely she'd been unable to leave this house. "Are you a slave in this household?" When she nodded, he asked, "What is your name?"

"I am Velaria of Ardennes."

"My name is Brian. I was raised in Penrith." When the men glanced over at them, Velaria lowered her head and moved to the next guest, filling his cup.

Brian took a sip of the wine, his mind spinning. This young woman needed help, and if he disappeared tonight, he might be able to get her out. Though it was dangerous, and he understood none of the language, he wanted to help her.

She turned back and met his gaze. In her expression, he saw the loss and hopelessness. He didn't know if he could find a way to buy her freedom. But perhaps this was Fate's way of granting him a second chance. He had failed to save Robert.

But maybe he could save her.

Brian waited until the men were sleeping, their bodies passed out from gluttony and drunkenness. In the darkness, he kept his footsteps light while he searched for the girl. Velaria wasn't anywhere in the stone kitchen, but he found a set of steps leading below ground.

She'd asked him to leave and find the Norman lord within the city. He was torn between trying to bring her with him or seeking help.

He decided to go down below to see if she was among the servants. Slowly, he crept down the stairs. An acrid stench assailed his nostrils, and he blinked into the darkness where only a single oil lamp was set into a stone crevice to offer light. Was this where Kadir kept his slaves?

Brian waited a moment for his eyes to adjust and saw rows of swords, maces, and daggers gleaming in the yellow light. He stepped closer and heard the clinking of chains.

Never would he forget that sound. The four of them—Piers, Robert, his sister Morwenna, and himself—had been captured by English soldiers after a raid at Penrith, years ago. They'd fought for their freedom . . . but Brian knew what it was to be kept in chains. Velaria was probably telling the truth. This was a place of captivity, not a place where they trained men to fight.

Brian crept back up the stairs, not daring to go any farther. He didn't know where Velaria was being held, but he would try to find the Norman lord within the city.

He slipped outside the house into the darkness. The night air had grown cooler, and he stopped to look for the Hagia Sophia. The church stood atop a hill, and he tried to remember the direction of the setting sun. Velaria had said to look for the door with three crosses. But the city was an endless maze of wooden houses, half of which had already burned down. He started walking toward the hill, hoping he would find the house from there.

The moon rose golden above Constantinople, illuminating the shadows of a nearby mosque. As Brian began to wander the streets, he saw dozens of beggars sleeping along the road while the scent of ruin and fire lingered.

Brian found a discarded torch and lit it from one of the dying fires in the city. As he continued to search for the lord's house, the voices of doubt intruded on him. *You've traveled nearly a thousand miles. And for what? To fail again?*

There were many people in this city who needed help, not just the girl. But as he continued walking, he couldn't stop thinking of Velaria. Despite her status as a slave, he sensed her bravery. Though she had tried to conceal her features by keeping her head lowered, she was quite pretty. Her blue eyes had captivated him, and he'd never met anyone like her.

Velaria had tried to warn him, and he was grateful for it. Had her family traveled on Crusade, or how had she come to be so far from England? And had her parents died? She seemed to be alone, like himself—but he wanted to help her.

His feet ached in the worn shoes, but he continued searching, house by house. He had been walking for nearly an hour when he suddenly heard dogs barking. At first, Brian didn't know what was happening, and he ducked into the shadows to stay out of their way. Then, he realized they were coming closer. He quickened his pace, moving down a narrow passageway—but the dogs seemed to follow.

They were tracking *him*, as if he were an escaped slave. Which seemed impossible for why would anyone go to such lengths to find him? He was a serf, not worth anything at all.

But the snarling grew louder, and he had to find somewhere to seek shelter. Brian hurried down another passageway, turning toward the outskirts of the city. By sheer luck, he found a doorway with three crosses marked upon it.

He took a deep breath and knocked on the door. The barking intensified, as if the dogs were coming closer. Brian pounded the door harder, hoping someone would answer. When no one did, he tried the door handle and it opened easily.

He moved inside and bolted it shut behind him. His heart raced while his lungs burned with fear. There was no one in the house—at least not that he could see. With his back against the door, he wondered whether Lord Staunton was here. And what could he say to the man?

An oil lamp flared, and a man staggered forward, the scent of wine permeating his skin and clothing. He spoke in the unfamiliar language, but Brian answered in English. "Velaria sent me to you. She said you could help. You are Lord Alexander of Staunton, are you not?"

At that, the man eyed him in disbelief. "I am, yes. But you've gone half-witted if you think I could help you." He shook his head. "Foolish boy. They despise us here." He came closer until he stared into Brian's eyes. "They want all crusaders dead after what our men did to the city."

A knock sounded at the door, and Brian begged, "Please. I will work for you. She is being held as a slave by Kadir al-Kumar. She needs your help."

At that, the Norman lord shook his head. "I can help no one, boy." He muttered beneath his breath. "They only allow me to live because of the bribes I've paid. The Byzantine fighters took my wife prisoner when we were trying to escape." After a long pause, he added, "She's gone now. But I will not rest until I've found her."

In his eyes, Brian saw the face of a man who was barely hanging on to his own survival. Baron Staunton had clearly loved his wife, and the resignation in his eyes didn't bode well. Brian didn't think there was anything he could say except, "I'm sorry." He lowered his voice and pleaded, "Will you let me hide here for the night? I'll leave at dawn, I promise."

Lord Staunton studied him for a moment. His expression turned bleak, and he shook his head. "I must answer the door, or they will break it down. There's nothing I can do for you, boy. But there's another door in the back. You can leave through there."

Disappointment and frustration shadowed Brian, but he had to seize his only chance at freedom. He hurried to the back of the house and found the narrow passageway, slipping outside just as the Norman lord opened the front door to answer. Brian didn't hear what the man said, but he kept his head down and hurried down the street.

As soon as he reached the end, two men were waiting. They seized him by his arms, and raw panic flooded through him. Brian reacted out of pure instinct, hardly aware of anything at all. Before they had a firm grasp, he twisted free, reaching for the blade at the first man's waist.

The world seemed to blur, and he remembered the training Robert had taught him. *Keep your balance. Be aware of your surroundings.*

He would not let them take him into slavery. Brian kept his eyes firmly on his enemies, remaining in a defensive stance while he glimpsed another street that could be an escape. Though he lacked a shield, the blade would be enough.

"So. You *do* know how to fight," came the voice of Kadir as he spoke English. The man stepped forward and regarded him. "That will be useful."

"I am leaving," Brian told him.

Kadir laughed. "You might escape for a time, boy. But every person in this city knows who I am. They won't hesitate to turn you in."

"I won't be your slave." He hadn't traveled all this way to lose his freedom.

When one of the men darted forward, Brian spun and slashed his arm. The man let out a foul curse, but Brian had his gaze locked upon his second opponent. He held steady for a moment before he bolted toward the other street. An invisible snare seemed to tighten around him, for he had no idea where he was going.

Just as he reached the edge of the city, a sharp pain blasted through his shoulder. An arrow had pierced him, and blood ran down his side.

His lungs burned as he struggled to keep running. But a small crowd gathered before him, closing in. They stared at him with hatred, and from behind, the dogs continued to track him.

Brian tried to turn in a different direction, but all around him, the beggars cut off his escape.

"You see?" Kadir's voice cut through the stillness. "They work for me. All the people of Constantinople know that I am generous to those who are loyal. And I punish any who disobey me."

The man moved in close, and when Brian tried to wield his blade, Kadir tore the arrow free. A cry broke forth, and Brian dropped to his knees from the brutal pain.

"I like your spirit, boy. You are fortunate that I do, for I will allow you to heal before I put you in my fighting pits."

Brian was hardly aware of Kadir's words as he was dragged to his feet, blood spilling from his shoulder.

"That spirit may be the only thing that keeps you alive, boy." He laughed again. "I hope you enjoyed your last night of freedom."

As they took him away, Brian glanced up at the moon, the bleakness settling into his bones.

Now he knew he would never see his sister again. But after everything he'd done, this was what he deserved.

If you enjoyed the excerpt, you can order *Her Warrior's Redemption* from a retailer of your choice!

Newsletter

If you enjoyed the story and would like to be notified when I have new books for sale, sign up for my newsletter at www.mic hellewillingham.com/contact. I only send out announcements of new books and special sales. Also, if you liked the book, please consider writing a review. These really help authors, so thank you so much!

If you want to read the other books in the MacKinloch Clan series, you can enjoy Claimed by the Highland Warrior (Bram and Nairna, Seduced by Her Highland Warrior (Alex and Laren), or Tempted by the Highland Warrior (Callum and Marguerite), available now wherever books are sold.

ALSO BY MICHELLE WILLINGHAM

The MacEgan Brothers Series

(Medieval Ireland)

*Her Warrior Captive (*formerly *Her Warrior Slave)*

"The Viking's Forbidden Captive" (novella, formerly "The Viking's Forbidden Love-Slave")

Her Warrior King

Her Irish Warrior

The Warrior's Touch

Taming Her Irish Warrior

"The Warrior's Forbidden Virgin" (novella)

"Voyage of an Irish Warrior" (novella)

Surrender to an Irish Warrior

"Pleasured by the Viking" (novella)

Warriors in Winter

The MacKinloch Clan Series

(Medieval Scotland)
Claimed by the Highland Warrior
Seduced by Her Highland Warrior
Tempted by the Highland Warrior
"Rescued by the Highland Warrior"

Sons of Sigurd

(Viking-era Ireland)
Stolen by the Viking
"The Viking's Redemption" (free prequel)

Secrets in Silk Series

(Regency Scotland)
Undone by the Duke
Unraveled by the Rebel
Undressed by the Earl
Unlaced by the Outlaw

The Earls Next Door Series

(Victorian England)
Good Earls Don't Lie
What the Earl Needs Now
The Taming of the Countess

Untamed Highlanders

(Regency Scotland/England)
The Highlander and the Governess
The Highlander and the Wallflower

Legendary Warriors Series

(Medieval Ireland)
The Iron Warrior Returns
The Untamed Warrior's Bride
Her Warrior's Redemption

Warriors of the Night Series

(Medieval England)
Forbidden Night with the Warrior
Forbidden Night with the Highlander
Forbidden Night with the Prince

School for Spinsters

(Regency England)
A Match Made in London
Match Me, I'm Falling
Match Me If You Can

Forbidden Vikings Series

(Viking-era Ireland)
To Sin with a Viking
To Tempt a Viking

Viking Voyagers

(Regency/Viking Time Travel)
A Viking for the Viscountess
A Viking Maiden for the Marquess

Warriors of Ireland Series

(Medieval Ireland)
Warrior of Ice
Warrior of Fire

Accidentally in Love Series

(Victorian England/Fictional Province of Lohenberg)
"An Accidental Seduction" (novella)
The Accidental Countess
The Accidental Princess
The Accidental Prince

Forbidden Weddings

(Regency England)
"A Dance with the Devil"
"The Sweetest Christmas"
"A Rake of Her Own"

Other Titles

"Innocent in the Harem"
"A Wish to Build a Dream On"

Contemporary Titles

(under the Avery Chandler pseudonym)
Christmas in His Arms
Switched at Marriage

About the Author

Kindle bestselling author and Rita® Award finalist **Michelle Willingham** has published nearly fifty romance novels and novellas. Currently, she lives in Virginia with her family and is working on more historical romance books in a variety of settings. When she's not writing, Michelle enjoys baking, playing the piano, and chasing after her cats. Her books have been translated into languages around the world and are also available in audio. Visit her website at www.michellewillingham.com.

www.ingramcontent.com/pod-product-compliance
Lightning Source LLC
Chambersburg PA
CBHW030004010826
48973CB00009B/2661